Dragon Lover

Also From Donna Grant

Don't miss these other spellbinding novels!

Dragon King Series
Dragon Revealed
Dragon Mine
Dragon Unbound
Dragon Eternal

Reaper Series
Dark Alpha's Claim
Dark Alpha's Embrace
Dark Alpha's Demand
Dark Alpha's Lover
Tall Dark Deadly Alpha Bundle
Dark Alpha's Night
Dark Alpha's Hunger
Dark Alpha's Awakening
Dark Alpha's Redemption
Dark Alpha's Temptation
Dark Alpha's Caress
Dark Alpha's Obsession
Dark Alpha's Need
Dark Alpha's Silent Night
Dark Alpha's Passion
Dark Alpha's Command

Skye Druid Series
Iron Ember

Kindred: The Fated Series
Rage

Dark King Series
Dark Heat (3 novella compilation)
Darkest Flame
Fire Rising

Burning Desire
Hot Blooded
Night's Blaze
Soul Scorched
Dragon King (novella)
Passion Ignites
Smoldering Hunger
Smoke And Fire
Dragon Fever (novella)
Firestorm
Blaze
Dragon Burn (novella)
Heat
Torched
Dragon Night (novella)
Dragonfire
Dragon Claimed (novella)
Ignite
Fever
Dragon Lost (novella)
Flame
Inferno
Whisky and Wishes (novella)
Heart of Gold (novella)
Of Fire and Flame (novella)
A Dragon's Tale (novella compilation)
A Warrior for Christmas

Kindred Series
Everkin
Eversong
Everwylde
Everbound
Evernight
Everspell

Dark Warrior Series
Midnight's Master
Midnight's Lover
Midnight's Seduction

Midnight's Warrior
Midnight's Kiss
Midnight's Captive
Midnight's Temptation
Midnight's Promise
Midnight's Surrender (novella)

Dark Sword Series
Dangerous Highlander
Forbidden Highlander
Wicked Highlander
Untamed Highlander
Shadow Highlander
Darkest Highlander

Rogues of Scotland Series
The Craving
The Hunger
The Tempted
The Seduced

Chiasson Series
Wild Fever
Wild Dream
Wild Need
Wild Flame
Wild Rapture

LaRue Series
Moon Kissed
Moon Thrall
Moon Bound
Moon Struck

Shield Series
A Dark Guardian
A Kind of Magic
A Dark Seduction
A Forbidden Temptation
A Warrior's Heart

Dragon Lover

A Dragon Kings Novella

By Donna Grant

1001 DARK NIGHTS

PRESS

Dragon Lover
A Dragon Kings Novella
By Donna Grant

1001 Dark Nights
Copyright 2023 Donna Grant
ISBN: 979-8-88542-009-9

Foreword: Copyright 2014 M. J. Rose

Published by 1001 Dark Nights Press, an imprint of Evil Eye Concepts, Incorporated

Acknowledgments from the Author

From the very first conversation with the phenomenal women at Evil Eye Publishing, I've been absolutely thrilled to publish, first the Dark Kings, and now the Dragon Kings series. I send out my heartfelt thanks to everyone involved in getting my books into the hands of readers.

A special thanks to the BETA readers who help keep things straight in my ever-growing Dark Universe. You all ROCK!

And to all of my ARC-Angels who are always ready and willing to read the Advanced Reader Copies and get reviews up on release day, you guys are the bomb!

Thank you to the DG Groupies who love to compare notes and try to guess what my characters are doing and where they might go next. I might not give away spoilers, but I love reading your comments.

To Charity, assistant, friend, mutual tea addict, and designer extraordinaire—THANK YOU!

One Thousand and One Dark Nights

Once upon a time, in the future…

*I was a student fascinated with stories and learning.
I studied philosophy, poetry, history, the occult, and
the art and science of love and magic. I had a vast
library at my father's home and collected thousands
of volumes of fantastic tales.*

*I learned all about ancient races and bygone
times. About myths and legends and dreams of all
people through the millennium. And the more I read
the stronger my imagination grew until I discovered
that I was able to travel into the stories… to actually
become part of them.*

*I wish I could say that I listened to my teacher
and respected my gift, as I ought to have. If I had, I
would not be telling you this tale now.
But I was foolhardy and confused, showing off
with bravery.*

*One afternoon, curious about the myth of the
Arabian Nights, I traveled back to ancient Persia to
see for myself if it was true that every day Shahryar
(Persian: شهريار, "king") married a new virgin, and then
sent yesterday's wife to be beheaded. It was written
and I had read that by the time he met Scheherazade,
the vizier's daughter, he'd killed one thousand
women.*

Something went wrong with my efforts. I arrived in the midst of the story and somehow exchanged places with Scheherazade – a phenomena that had never occurred before and that still to this day, I cannot explain.

Now I am trapped in that ancient past. I have taken on Scheherazade's life and the only way I can protect myself and stay alive is to do what she did to protect herself and stay alive.

Every night the King calls for me and listens as I spin tales. And when the evening ends and dawn breaks, I stop at a point that leaves him breathless and yearning for more. And so the King spares my life for one more day, so that he might hear the rest of my dark tale.

As soon as I finish a story... I begin a new one... like the one that you, dear reader, have before you now.

Chapter One

On top of a small outcropping of flat rocks high atop a mountain, Kendrick sat with his legs dangling over the side, awed by the sunrise. *Beautiful.* The thought went through his mind every time he saw the sun break over the mountains. He leaned back on his hands and smiled.

"It really is stunning. Whether I'm on Zora or Earth, it's a sight to behold. They're nearly identical, though you'll have to take my word for it." He paused and looked over his shoulder into the small cave behind him.

A loud sigh came from within.

Kendrick's enhanced vision cut through the shadows to the small dragon inside. He'd been surprised and thrilled to discover that a Pink had a home in the region he'd been assigned to patrol. Dragons tended to stay away from the borders of their considerable-sized domain simply because they didn't want to encounter humans of any kind.

Despite Kendrick's weeks on Zora, the Pink had yet to speak to him. Kendrick wasn't giving up, though. He, like the other Dragon Kings, had long feared that the Pinks had been wiped out during the war on Earth with the mortals. Once the Kings came to Zora, they saw the dragons they hadn't seen in eons flourishing—and with them, the Pinks.

The tiniest of dragon species were known to be aloof, but this one in particular took it to a whole new level. Not that Kendrick could blame her. It wasn't just this dragon, either. None of the dragons on Zora were thrilled to see the Kings.

Kendrick frowned as the past barreled through the carefully constructed walls within his mind. He sighed and looked back at the sun. "It's easy to look at someone's mistakes and criticize things. It wasna so black and white. Things were...difficult back then."

Difficult. Ha. That was an understatement. Things on Earth had been hell. It didn't seem to matter what the Kings did, the humans were never happy. With every new truce, there was retaliation—from both sides.

No one knew who started it. The blame couldn't be placed at the feet of the dragons or the mortals. The Kings had done what they thought was right.

And it had led to them losing *everything*.

Kendrick squeezed his eyes shut as the bleak, treacherous emotions he kept locked away broke loose. He hated delving into the past. There was nothing there but rage, resentment, and despair. He ran his hands down his face in a bid to lock the past away, but he didn't quite manage it. He opened his eyes and scanned the horizon. His area to patrol was breathtaking. A magnificent mountain range with stunning vistas, valleys filled with a lush forest, and a wide lake. Across the invisible border was a vast grassland. And beyond that, a plateau.

On his many flights, Kendrick had seen the enormous size of the plateau and the mountains that rose behind it. He'd be lying if he said that he wasn't interested in exploring the land across the border. But the Kings had already run into trouble by doing just that.

The situation with the mortals on the west side of dragon land in the city of Stonemore had taken a drastic turn with the disappearance of one of theirs—Merrill. It likely meant that war was on the horizon. The Kings were used to being the biggest, most dangerous entities on Earth, but they had recently learned that something on Zora could take down even a King. The new foe was why the other Kings were on the realm and actively guarding the borders.

Kendrick wanted to find the new adversary. He wasn't worried about encountering it, regardless of how easily the enemy had taken down other Kings. It would be caught—and killed. It was only a matter of time. What weighed so heavily on Kendrick's mind was Merrill. He knew his friend. Merrill was astute and cunning.

If someone had taken Merrill as they had with Varek, the Kings would find them. And dole out their brand of justice. Some thought Merrill had left on his own, much as Brandr had, but Kendrick didn't buy that. Neither did Varek, Merrill's best friend. That left only one other possibility. And Kendrick refused to consider that his friend's life had been taken.

Movement to his left drew Kendrick's attention. He watched as the Pink emerged from her cave. She shook and stretched gracefully, unfurling one wing and then the other before tucking them against her sleek body. The Pinks had rounded scales that gave them a harder shell than any other dragon. Small fan-like growths ran down their spines. And a Pink's tail was particularly dangerous, ending in a flat, fan-like tip that held sharp barbs as hard as a dragon's talons.

"Why are you out here on your own?" Kendrick had asked her the same question every day since being assigned to the territory. He had yet to get an answer. "I know you can understand me. Whether I speak like this"—he paused and opened the mental link to talk telepathically as all dragons did—"*or like this.*"

The Pink turned and looked at him for a moment, her emerald eyes flashing. Instead of flying off, she simply sat and gazed at the scenery. After a stretch of silence, Kendrick did the same.

"We failed you on Earth. You have a second chance here, and we're going to make sure we doona repeat the mistakes of the past." Kendrick thought of Shaw and Cullen and their run-in with humans who now knew dragons had crossed onto their land. They seemed to be on the precipice of the war the twins, Brandr and Eurwen, had spent thousands of years ensuring never happened.

Could they keep such a promise and keep it at bay? Brandr and Eurwen had gone to great lengths to ensure the mortals stayed away from the dragons and vice versa. The twins hadn't wanted any of the Kings on Zora initially—mostly because they had issues with their father, Constantine, King of Dragon Kings.

In the end, Eurwen had granted Con and the twins' mother, Rhi, access to Zora. Kendrick wondered if Con and Rhi would have been allowed to come had Varek not been kidnapped and brought to the realm. In the end, their new adversary's attack propelled the twins to agree to let some of the Kings help contain the situation.

It should've been easy. They should've caught the enemy quickly. But that didn't happen. Mainly because the foe managed to make itself invisible. It was difficult to locate and defeat if no one could see it.

Kendrick hadn't given up looking, though, and the twins had finally issued an open invitation to the realm. Which was a good thing since a few of his brethren had found their mates on this new world. Not to mention, Eurwen and Brandr would need help if the war did happen. Cullen and Shaw had done what they could to keep things from escalating, but those who ruled Stonemore were killing anyone with magic—especially children. Someone had to put a halt to it, and that's what the Kings had done. Unfortunately, it hadn't occurred covertly.

Kendrick grinned as his thoughts turned to happier subjects. Namely Varek and his warrior mate, Jeyra. "You should've seen the mating ceremony," he told the Pink. "Or maybe you did. It was a spectacular event. If you missed it, you'll have a chance to see others, I'm sure. Cullen and Tamlyn will eventually have their ceremony. My bet is that they're next to make things official. Tamlyn is a Banshee. Did I tell you that already?"

The Pink rolled her eyes.

Kendrick held back his grin. "Ah. So I did. What about Shaw and Nia? She was held as a slave in Stonemore, a city built into the side of the mountain. I hear it's quite a sight." His smile vanished, thinking of the city that held so much blood and death. "That's the last place Merrill was seen. He and Shaw went there to stop the humans from killing children with magic."

There should've been more than two Kings at Stonemore. If there had been, someone would have been watching the other two's backs in case something happened—which it had.

Kendrick opened his mental link again. *"Merrill? Just let me know you're all right, brother. Please."*

But like every day since Merrill had disappeared, there was no reply.

Kendrick glanced at the Pink to find her studying him. Just as he opened his mouth to talk, the Pink jerked her gaze away. Her entire body grew rigid as her look intensified. She slowly stood, a low growl emanating from her. Kendrick followed her line of sight. He saw nothing, no matter how hard he tried. Suddenly, out of the corner of his eye, he saw what looked like a ripple.

It was just how Shaw, Brandr, and Eurwen had described the new enemy before it struck. Kendrick immediately got to his feet. It was here. His heart rate increased as anticipation rushed through him.

"I've got the bastard," he murmured.

The Pink made a sound. Kendrick ignored her and shifted into his true form. He dove from the rock and spread his wings to soar toward the location. The Pink darted in front of him, her tiny wings flapping rapidly to keep up. When he didn't heed her, she began bumping into him.

"I must," he told her.

When she didn't relent, he flew faster, leaving her behind. This adversary had caused enough harm. Someone needed to stop it. He was the closest. It would be foolish to wait for others and risk losing this enemy again.

Kendrick angled himself to see out of the corner of his eye. He flew back and forth over the area without seeing anything. Frustration churned in his stomach. Just as he was about to fly away, he saw the ripple again. This time, he wouldn't let the entity get away.

Despite believing he had locked on to the adversary, Kendrick lost it a second time. He didn't hesitate to act when he spotted it the third time. He dove to tackle it. He didn't slow, even as he passed through the barrier of dragon land and moved into the human side of the territory. He *would* catch his opponent.

With his wings tucked against his body and the wind whipping past him in a rush, Kendrick released a breath of fire. It scorched the earth where he was sure the enemy had been. He was just circling back for a second attack when something slammed into him. The next thing he knew, he crashed into the ground in human form. Bones snapped at the force of the impact.

Kendrick hadn't shifted, he was certain of that. He pushed up onto one elbow as the world spun and his bones knitted back together. His body…fuck. It hurt in ways he'd never experienced. The pain was so debilitating that he nearly passed out. He shook from the agony and the magic that had struck him. His stomach heaved, but he fought for control.

He shook his head to clear it, but that only made things worse. His enhanced hearing caught a whisper of a sound. Was it his enemy? Or a new one? It didn't matter. He had to get up and face it. He got to his feet on unsteady limbs and called clothes to his nakedness. He staggered, doing everything he could to stay upright—which shouldn't be so difficult.

Kendrick knew he wasn't alone. His senses warned him that something was closing in, and fast. He kept his gaze on the horizon to combat the dizziness. That allowed him to concentrate on his peripheral vision to catch a glimpse of the enemy again.

This time, just as he braced for an attack from the side, the magic hit him square in the chest. The agony that radiated through Kendrick snatched his breath. He landed hard, something dark and cloying engulfing him before he knew what had happened. It felt as if something were invading his skin and trying to rip his muscles apart and shatter his bones systematically. With gritted teeth, he fought against the rising tide of pain.

Kendrick tried to shift again, but he couldn't. The sheer terror that assaulted him made him panic for an instant. He then resorted to magic, fighting any way he could. Each time he started to heal, whatever had a hold of him struck again. Worse was the residual magic that lingered. He even thought he heard a laugh near his ear.

The enemy was on him, around him, and *still*, Kendrick couldn't see what it was. He bellowed and released more magic. It was enough to get away from the entity. Kendrick knew it would return, but he would be upright when it did. It was getting harder and harder to stay on his feet, but he refused to fall.

He tried again to shift now that he was free of the foe's energy. When he couldn't, panic stole over him. Cullen had warned him about this. So had Brandr and Eurwen, but he hadn't listened. He'd believed things would be different for him, and look where that had gotten him. He'd been too intent on taking down their adversary, and now, he would pay the price.

He felt a slight shift in the air. Kendrick looked out of the corner of his eye and saw the ripple once more. He dove to the side and then rolled to his feet. A grin split his face when he realized he'd dodged the assault. He turned to use his peripheral vision for the next attack. It came from above this time, pounding into him so hard that his legs buckled.

"Not as powerful as you thought, are you?"

The disembodied voice filled the area around him. Kendrick lifted his head as his body swiftly mended. The entity was toying with him. Fury burned within him. If that was how this thing wanted to play, then he was game. Kendrick climbed to his feet and attempted once more to shift. It took everything he had to hold back the panic that lodged itself in his chest when he couldn't.

He was a Dragon King. He had fought many wars, gone up against some of the most powerful beings, and had come out on top. He wasn't afraid of death. The magic of Earth had chosen him to lead his clan, and nothing on this realm or any other would make him stop fighting.

Kendrick took a deep breath and released it. He then smiled. "I wouldna worry about me."

He saw a ripple out of the corner of his eye. Kendrick spun away, but he was too slow. The magic enveloped him. It stuck to his skin, seeped into every pore as if it were suffocating him. This wasn't the end. Was it? A King could only be killed by another King. Unless this *was* a Dragon King, and they didn't know it.

That thought was a sobering one. Kendrick should've told Con and the others what he was doing. He should've waited for them. Whatever he fought believed it was stronger. It thought it could take him down. And while it had an advantage, everything had a weakness. Kendrick just needed to find what that was.

He called to his magic, but it was slow to respond. That's when Kendrick realized the entity was causing this. He stopped fighting what held him and concentrated on his magic instead. It moved slowly, but it did answer him this time. He gathered it and let it build until he finally released it.

In an instant, he was free. His limbs froze as he dropped to his knees. Kendrick gathered more magic, ready to fight off the next attack, when he heard a war cry. The entity might have released him, but the residual magic was unrelenting. He heard footsteps and looked up to find warriors gathered around something to his left. His gaze landed on a female who moved with such speed and grace that he stared in wonder for a moment. She swung her sword effortlessly.

He willed the lingering effects of the attack to dissipate as he got to his feet. And with a smile, he called his sword and joined her and the others.

Chapter Two

Esha paused with her fellow Rangers to locate the being. After several moments, she realized it was gone. With a curse, she lowered her sword. That was when she remembered the human. She turned to face him.

He looked the worse for wear. His clothes—items she wasn't familiar with—were torn and dirty from the scuffle. The simple shirt of royal blue looked too thin to protect him from anything, and his black pants were made of a thick material that she imagined made it impossible for him to move easily. However, she liked his thick-soled boots, though they looked heavy. His longish, wavy, black hair now held twigs and debris. Dirt smudged his face, but it was his vivid green eyes that caught and held hers.

When the call came that someone had spotted the entity, Esha hadn't hesitated to take her squad after it. She had been shocked to find the human engaged in combat with it. They had encountered the presence before, and she had lost two Rangers during the confrontation. How had this human survived?

With a glance, she silently told her team to keep a lookout in case the entity returned. Esha didn't sheathe her sword. She glanced at the trampled grass. The attack had covered a considerable area. She returned her gaze to the man. He was tall, his shoulders broad, and his face fair. He carried himself and the sword in his hand as if he were well acquainted with battle. It wasn't that she hadn't seen a handsome human before, but something about this one was different—something that wouldn't let her look away.

Black brows slashed over his eyes. His nose was straight, his jaw firm. He had wide lips that were almost too full for a man. Suddenly, that mouth quirked up at the corners, which made her frown. She lifted her gaze back to his.

"How did you get here?" she demanded.

He tilted his head to the side.

She repeated the question.

He blinked.

The closest city was Rannora. He should know that language, but by the look on his face, it appeared he didn't. She parted her lips, ready to ask in another language.

He responded in perfect Rannoran, "I walked."

Esha snorted. "From Rannora? I'll ask again. How did you get here?"

"Who are you?"

"The head of the Asavori Rangers."

Damn if he didn't grin wider. "Do you have a name?"

Everyone knew her name. She frowned. He didn't look like any of the humans she had seen at Rannora or in Belanore. "If you know Rannoran, then you know the Rangers. Which means you should know who I am." He was either teasing her or…he wasn't from either city. She strode to him and put the point of her blade to his throat. "Who are you? How did you get here?"

"My name is Kendrick. I came from there."

He nodded to where the border of the dragon land lay. She glanced into the distance to find the boundary quite a distance away. "You're lying."

"I doona lie."

He said it in the language of the humans but with an accent she didn't recognize. Around her, the team watched, waiting for her to make a decision.

Kendrick lifted his hands, palms out. "I take it you saw me being attacked?"

He had switched back to Rannoran easily. "Speak in your tongue," she snapped. He left her disconcerted, and it wasn't a good feeling.

"I've been tracking the thing I was fighting."

She pressed the tip of her sword into his skin, causing a bead of blood to appear. "You? A human? You expect me to believe that?"

He studied her, almost as if weighing how to reply. "Did your eyes deceive you?"

No, dammit, they hadn't. "The fighting is usually left to us." She paused, searching his face and looking for any signs of deceit, but she didn't find anything. Esha lowered her sword. "Return the way you came."

"I can no'."

She glared at him. "It wasn't a suggestion."

"I need to find that being."

"Don't worry about it. We'll take care of it," she said and turned away.

"I'm afraid that isna good enough."

Esha spun back to find he had followed her. She lifted her sword again, but he didn't back away as others usually did. "It will have to be."

"I'm going to keep hunting," Kendrick said.

Esha was about to force him onto dragon land. If he lied, then the dragons could take care of him. The simple fact that he stood before her seemingly unhurt made her reevaluate the situation. He'd survived the attack. He might be able to share something that could help her people. It would behoove her to find out before she made him leave. "Did you track it?"

"Aye."

"Can you see it?"

"If I look out of the corner of my eye."

She nodded. That was how they saw it, as well.

"There's also a shift in the air before it attacks," he said.

Now that was something new. Esha pressed her lips together. Something about this stranger set her teeth on edge. He was too calm, too confident when faced with a squad of Rangers. Still, she couldn't help but consider that he might be able to assist them. They had been trying to find the being for weeks without any luck.

"I can help," Kendrick said. "We could work together."

Ryul snickered, then cut Kendrick a look, his gold eyes narrowed with disgust. "You're not a Ranger. We don't work with outsiders."

Esha agreed, but the adversary they had been tracking had left a trail of death in its wake. Dozens from both cities had been killed. The Rangers had been struggling to locate the entity for weeks without any success—until today.

The only difference was Kendrick, whoever he might be. Only a fool would send him off without using him. Esha hadn't gotten her position by doing foolish things, and she wasn't going to start now.

"Your weapon wasn't much use," she said. "You didn't have it when we came upon you."

"I have it now," he replied.

She eyed him before she lowered her sword. He knew he wasn't being completely honest, but she couldn't determine what he was hiding or why. She wasn't worried about him attacking them. They were Asavori Rangers, after all. Each of them had spent decades training before joining a crew. If he attacked one of them, the rest would take him out within seconds.

"You're very sure of yourself," she retorted.

He shrugged. "No more so than you or your warriors."

Esha decided to take the decision out of her hands. "Someone else will decide your fate. Come."

Kendrick smiled in response when others would've been quaking in their shoes—more proof that he wasn't from their land of Shecrish. If he had come from Idrias across the border, then how had he survived the dragons? Or was he working with the entity he claimed to track?

"You may not be smiling when this is finished," she told him.

Kendrick shrugged. "Lead the way."

Ryul took point as they headed out. Esha brought up the rear. Kendrick fell into step with her. After several minutes, she couldn't take his sidelong looks any longer.

"What is it?" she bit out.

His nose wrinkled. "My apologies. I've never seen anyone with ears like yours."

"You mean you've never seen an elf." It came out harsher than intended.

"Nay."

There was no way he could be from Shecrish and have not seen an elf. That could only mean…shite. Was he really from Idrias? Did that mean the dragons were gone as the rumors suggested?

Esha was suddenly self-conscious of her pointed ears sticking out of her hair. When she glanced at Kendrick, he was looking from one Ranger to another. Then his green gaze swung back to her.

"I didna know elves existed," he admitted.

"You'll see many elves in Shecrish. There are a few mortals like you, but not many."

"Shecrish? Is that a city?"

"Our area of land. It extends from the border where we found you, across to the far mountains to the east, up to the mountains in the north, and down to the sea in the south."

He nodded. "Do you no' approve of humans?"

"It isn't that. It's more…" She paused, searching for the right word. "They don't always agree with how elves live. We have our own ways that differ greatly from the humans'."

Kendrick's gaze moved to the plateau that loomed before them. "What do you do with those who wish to leave?"

"We send them to places where they will find those like themselves."

"Do elves have magic?"

She eyed him. "Aye. Many different kinds."

"Do the humans in Shecrish have magic?"

"Some."

"Do you…allow it?"

Esha jerked her head to him and frowned, taken aback. "What a curious question."

"It isna. No' if you know what I do."

"And what is that?"

He held her gaze. "Some are killing those with magic."

She couldn't comprehend such an act. "I dare them to come here, then. We *are* magic."

"Good. That's verra good." Kendrick's lips curled into a soft smile.

They walked for a while in silence. She noticed how he kept glancing at the plateau and the many waterfalls that fell from it. She watched him as they drew closer. Esha knew the instant he noticed the carved elves by the way he stopped and stared. She looked up at the creations where water fell from the mouths of the statues. The enormous figures were only on the west side of the plateau, set over a thousand meters apart.

"Beautiful," he murmured.

Esha inwardly smiled. She had always thought so, too. No matter how often she saw the Sentinels, as her people called them, she never grew tired of the sight.

"Who carved them?"

She shrugged. "We don't know. We call them the Sentinels."

"What is the name of the plateau?" he asked as he looked at her.

"The Corrial Plateau. The mountains to the east are the Dangerous Peaks."

"Interesting name."

"They aren't a place you want to go."

Kendrick returned his gaze to the waterfalls. "Water must be plentiful in the plateau."

"It rains nearly every day."

"I see."

She glanced to where the group had gotten ahead. "The land is full of dangers."

"They usually are," he murmured.

Ryul looked back at her, eyeing Kendrick with displeasure, but he said nothing. Esha knew she would have to come up with something convincing when they reached Flamefall. She might lead the Rangers, but she still answered to another. That someone just happened to be her sister, Savita. It was extremely rare for a guest to enter their sanctuary.

"Would it help if I were tied?"

She glanced at Kendrick. It was obvious he had paid attention to what was going on around him. "No."

"I can wait here until you speak to whoever it is who will decide my fate."

That would be a better solution than taking a stranger into their camp. Esha motioned for Kendrick to follow her. She looked at each of the five females and four males of her team, trying to determine who to leave with Kendrick.

They all followed her. They were all loyal. But she could see they weren't sure of her decision. How could she tell them that her gut told her Kendrick could help? He was a human, and humans relied on elves. Would she really ask her Rangers to trust a mortal? It was absurd.

Esha waited until they had reached the base of the plateau before she made her decision. "Zentha, take half the squad and head to camp. The rest of us will wait here for your return with Savita."

Zentha hesitated for just a second before she bowed her head of dark brown hair and called out half the squad to accompany her. Once they were gone, Esha turned to Kendrick. He stood at the edge of the pool at the base of one of the waterfalls. His head was tilted back to stare up at the cascading falls and the carving. Then he looked down at the bright blue waters below. When he turned back to her, she noted that his face and clothes were clean and repaired. Now she understood why he was pleased that they didn't retaliate against those with magic.

"What kind of magic do you have?" she asked.

Kendrick twisted his lips. "All kinds."

"Then a better question would be: What are you?"

A flicker of something passed over his face. "I'm a friend. This I vow."

"We'll find out," she warned. "But it would be better if you told me now."

He took a deep breath, his shoulders rising before he exhaled. "I'm a dragon."

Chapter Three

Kendrick should've been prepared for the disbelief reflected in Esha's golden-amber eyes, but he was still shocked by it. He'd been worried about telling her who he was, debated with himself about lying. But if he were going to convince her that they should hunt their mutual foe together, he decided that honesty was best. Now, he wondered if he'd made a mistake.

He thought about showing her, but then he remembered not being able to shift after his skirmish. He was still shaken by that encounter and everything he'd experienced. He'd had time to think about it as they traveled toward the plateau, and he was no closer to saying what he'd fought. Their travels had also given his body time to deal with the remaining residual magic. Yet his three unsuccessful attempts to shift left him concerned that the entity might have changed him permanently.

Their long trek had given him something else, as well—time to study the intriguing and beautiful warrior who had dared to put her blade against his throat. Kendrick was well acquainted with the human portrayal of elves on Earth in every form of entertainment there was, but he had never encountered one before. He'd thought them pure fiction. Until he stood before not just one but nearly a dozen.

He had so many questions, and it was difficult to keep from asking them. He doubted Esha would share much until she knew she could trust him. The elves around him had different coloring, and though he tried not to stare, he couldn't help his curiosity.

Worse, he couldn't stop ogling Esha. From the moment his gaze landed on her, he had been utterly transfixed. She was on the taller side of average, and the way she moved with such fluid motions when she fought suggested that she was far from new to battle. Her brown skin had a golden glow in the sun that almost made it appear as if she were sprinkled with gold dust. He longed to sink his fingers into the wavy length of her tawny hair that reminded him of a lion's coat with two thick braids on either side of her head that were then gathered into one braid that fell with the rest of her locks past her shoulders. Pointed ears protruded from her hair. Her right ear had a piercing near the tip with a chain attached to a tiny cuff lower down.

His gaze moved to her oval face. Her delicate features consisted of a small nose, plump lips with the lower more pronounced, and captivating, golden-amber, almond-shaped eyes. Those eyes watched him curiously now.

The markings on her face intrigued him. Small white dots followed the curve of each brow. In the middle of her forehead was a circle of white about the size of a dime with eight lines protruding from it. A thin white line started at her cheek and faded near her temple.

She wore a simple cream shirt that was both functional and somehow sexy. A leather corset with four buckles molded her body from just under her breasts to her hips. Leather vambraces with a beautiful golden design protected her forearms. Trousers of deep brown covered her legs, hugging them like a second skin and allowing her to move easily. Plain leather boots covered her feet up to her knees. A leather strap hung at her hips, where she had a dagger tied to her right thigh. Another harness lay across her body, her sword resting at her back in its scabbard.

Esha quirked a brow at his perusal before going to speak to the other elves. A couple had her coloring. Kendrick couldn't wait to learn everything about them. His brethren would be excited about receiving information on the elves. That thought made him flinch, a reminder that he hadn't told anyone where he was. It would be wise to contact Con immediately. With Merrill missing, he didn't want anyone worried about him.

But if he told Con where he was now, their King would likely order him back to his section to patrol—not that he would blame Con. But this was a prime opportunity to learn about others on Zora—those he was sure Eurwen and Brandr knew nothing about. Not to mention gathering whatever knowledge they had on the thing he'd fought. He would give himself a little more time before checking in with Con and the others. It wasn't as if he couldn't get away from the Rangers anytime he wanted.

Kendrick made himself look away from the elves. He turned to the sheer face of the plateau. How many times had he looked at it from across the border? His eyesight allowed him to see farther than most beings, but it had been too far away for him to pick up the carvings in the rockface.

He leaned his head back. The faces were so distinct, he could make out the individual features of each one. After the water fell from their open mouths, the carvings faded, almost as if whoever had created them was more concerned with the heads than anything else. Regardless, it was a remarkable, eye-catching structure. Esha had called them the Sentinels. Yes, he could see that. They appeared to watch over the western side of the land. Were there other such faces around the plateau? He was dying to find out.

Kendrick followed the long fall of water to the pool that it crashed into. Mist shrouded the lower part of the plateau as the water churned white from the dramatic fall before rippling out to showcase a stunning cobalt pool.

The roar of the waterfalls was loud though strangely calming. He didn't lower his guard because only a fool would do that, but he paused and took stock of his body, something he hadn't done since the skirmish. He was sore, but he had healed any damage. The fact that remnants of pain lingered was worrying.

He had dismissed his friends' warnings about tangling with the unknown adversary to his detriment. Kendrick wasn't entirely certain that he would've come out of it unscathed if Esha and the Rangers hadn't appeared. On Earth, they knew that only a Dragon King could kill a Dragon King. That gave all Kings the confidence to face all foes without fear of death. But Zora wasn't Earth, and Kendrick had been reckless in not remembering that.

They had no idea what this thing they were after was or what it could do. It had killed multiple dragons, and it'd taken down several Kings. Yet Kendrick had thoughtlessly shoved that knowledge aside and raced after it. All because he'd been in an irksome mood and wanted to take it out on someone.

Merrill's disappearance frightened him, and if something happened to *him*, Kendrick would cause his brethren the same worry and pain. That wasn't the dragon he was. He needed to get his shite together. Quick.

"You look deep in thought."

His head swiveled to the side at the sound of Esha's voice. She spoke English with a slight accent that he couldn't quite place. The language she had spoken before was lilting and flowed easily, reminding him of Finnish. Once he caught a sound similar to that language, he was able to understand it easily—though Esha hadn't seemed thrilled by that. She stuck with English now.

"Aye," he said.

She released a breath. "I took a chance bringing you here. Outsiders aren't welcome."

"Then why did you bring me?"

"Because you survived the attack. I've seen what that thing can do to my Rangers. Yet you're not only standing but appear unharmed."

Kendrick thought about the soreness that plagued him, something that would never have remained before. "I wouldna say I am no' injured."

"You seem hale and hearty."

He chuckled and glanced at the water. "I'll admit, I've never fought anything like that before. It was more than no' being able to see it. It was as if…"

"It knew what you were going to do?"

"Aye." He nodded, holding her gaze. "How many times have you tangled with it?"

Her lips flattened for a heartbeat. "This was my second time. It isn't easy to track, and we're experts."

"We've found the same thing."

That got her attention. "How many times have you fought it?"

"This was my first time personally. My friends have encountered it four other times."

"Did you lose anyone?"

Kendrick thought about the dragons and the moving burial. "We did."

"Where are your friends now? Across the border?"

He heard the mockery in her voice and fought his smile. "Is it so impossible for you to believe I'm a dragon?"

"Do you know how many dragons I've seen in my lifetime?"

"I doona know. Maybe a dozen? Two dozen?"

"None," she stated flatly.

Kendrick searched her amber gaze and saw the truth of her words. "I gather you doona spend time near the border."

"Not because I fear it. We're needed elsewhere around Shecrish. There has been talk among my people for generations that the dragons are gone."

That was concerning. Kendrick knew the dragons didn't go near their borders because they didn't want to see humans, but maybe it was time they did just that. Not to mention, he had been patrolling for several weeks. Surely, someone saw him. "What keeps you from crossing the border?"

She shrugged one shoulder. "Fear."

He hoped that would be enough to keep her people out. If it wasn't, there was a good chance a second war would be on the dragons' doorstep. Bloody hell.

"Obviously, if you've come from Idrias, then the dragons are gone."

"Idrias?"

"It's what we call the land of the dragons."

Kendrick held her gaze and looked intently at her as he said, "I'm no' lying, Esha. I am a dragon."

"You look very human to me."

"Because I want to appear that way."

Her brows shot up. "So, you claim to be a shapeshifter now? How many forms can you take?"

"Just two."

She snorted. "Shapeshifters aren't real. They're a myth created to scare children into doing as their parents say."

Her words floored Kendrick. All this time, he'd thought elves were a myth. She believed he was. A part of him wanted to shift right then and see what she did. However, he wasn't entirely certain she and the other Rangers wouldn't attack. He had no idea if the elves could hurt him or what type of damage remained from his earlier battle. He would show her his true self, but not yet.

Esha took a step toward him. "My advice is to speak only the truth when Savita arrives. She'll be able to discern if you aren't."

"I've spoken only the truth with you."

Her face darkened with ire. "Do you have any idea what will happen if Savita decides you can't be of help? I could be forced to kill you."

"You brought me because you saw the potential of us working together against a common enemy."

Esha shook her head and rested her hand on the hilt of her dagger. "I'm questioning myself now."

"Because it's too impossible to believe I'm what I say I am? What if I told you, until today, I didna think elves existed?"

She shrugged. "We go to great pains to bring other elves here. They wouldn't fit in elsewhere."

"How do you know that? Have you seen other places on this realm?"

"No."

He shrugged. "My point exactly. Who has?"

"We don't go to get our people."

Kendrick considered her words for a moment. "That means you send someone else to do it. Or…you use magic."

Esha smiled at his last words. "Our magic is extensive. I'd suggest you keep that in mind."

"Oh, I will, lass."

She frowned at him. "What is a *lass?*"

"Just a word that means a woman."

Esha turned when someone called her name. Kendrick followed the sound and saw that Zentha had returned with another female whose gaze was locked on him. The woman had the same golden-brown skin as Esha. Her straight, tawny hair was parted down the middle and hung to her hips.

There was a large gold sun painted in the middle of the woman's forehead. Her lower lashes had a band of gold running from the outer corners of her eyes outward to her temple. Five gold dots followed the line of each collarbone.

She wore a long, flowing, sleeveless gown of white, tied with a golden belt at her waist. A gold-colored stole draped over each arm, the length of the ends nearly touching the ground. She walked with purposeful steps as she made her way to him. She looked like a holy woman, and everyone clearly revered her.

He watched as Esha greeted the woman, speaking softly. He suspected the new arrival was Savita. The two shared a few words before the woman's gaze returned to him. So, this was who would determine if he was lying—and decide his fate.

He bowed his head in greeting, waiting patiently for the inevitable barrage of questions. He'd already decided how he would answer one in particular. He just hoped they were ready for his response.

Chapter Four

Esha smiled at her sister. She and Savita had been raised with the same couple, and since there were no blood relatives on their realm, Savita was the closest thing she had to family.

"He's...certainly interesting to look at," Savita said.

Esha straightened and glanced over her shoulder at Kendrick. "He is."

"Did he really fight the entity?"

"We came upon them in battle."

"Did this mortal beat it?"

Esha hesitated. "No. That isn't why I brought him. Look at him, sister. He isn't wounded. He was slow to get up, but he has recovered quickly."

"That's what Zentha told me, as well." Savita pressed her lips together as her gaze returned to Esha. "You want to bring him, a human, to Flamefall?"

"Absolutely, not. But he did have a point. We have a common enemy. He found the entity. It might have been luck, or perhaps he knows something we don't. As much as it pains me to admit, we've had difficulties tracking this thing. I think it would be prudent to work with him."

Savita was silent for a long moment. "You might have a point. Tell me more about him. Where is he from? Zentha said you found him near the border to Idrias."

Esha had been dreading this. She sighed. "He claims to come from there."

"So the dragons are gone?" Savita said, her eyes twinkling with interest. "The Conclave will love to know that."

"Actually, he says he *is* a dragon."

Savita's smile vanished in an instant. "Does he truly think he can attempt to convince us he's a shapeshifter? Everyone knows they don't exist."

"He can do magic."

"You saw it?"

Esha blew out a breath. "No, but he repaired his clothing."

"That's simple magic. Shapeshifting is something altogether different."

"There's more. He can speak Rannoran as well as if he were born there."

"How?" Savita demanded, her brows furrowed.

Esha shrugged. "He didn't say. Someone from Rannora must have made their way across the border and taught him."

Now that Esha was repeating everything, it sounded preposterous to her ears. Yet she couldn't help looking at Kendrick again and wondering, *what if?*

Savita walked around her. Esha followed her sister to where Kendrick waited at the pool. He greeted Savita with a hand on his chest as he inclined his head. She looked him up and down, no doubt noting that his garments differed from theirs.

"My name is Savita. It's my job to determine what is best for the Rangers."

Kendrick clasped his hands behind his back. "It's nice to meet you, Savita. I'm Kendrick. Esha and her team came to my aid earlier."

"Against the thing we've been trying to kill. Yes, I heard." Savita raked her eyes up and down him. "That creature has wreaked havoc across our lands. We aim to stop it."

"That is our goal, as well."

Savita lifted a brow. "You say *our*, yet you're alone. Where are the rest of your people?"

"Waiting to hear from me."

"You also claim to come from Idrias."

Kendrick glanced at Esha. "I doona claim it. It's fact."

"No one saw you come from that land."

"I've no idea if they did or didna. I was intent on my quarry."

Savita changed the subject quickly. "How do you speak Rannoran?"

His lips twisted ruefully. "I pick up languages quickly."

"Is that so?"

Esha knew what was coming. She didn't understand the need within her to demand her sister stop. She didn't understand anything she had done since encountering Kendrick. She couldn't explain her thoughts or reasonings, and it confounded her. Esha bit her tongue to keep herself silent even as Savita began to speak in Belanorise. Esha's gaze locked on Kendrick. She saw his laser focus as he listened to Savita. By the third sentence, he seemed to relax.

Kendrick replied in the same language. "I am no liar. I speak the truth, and you have no reason to call my mother names since you know nothing of her."

Esha released a breath she hadn't realized she had been holding. She glanced at Savita to find her sister's face slack with shock. It wasn't every day that a Reader was drawn up short like that.

"Would you like to try another?" Kendrick asked in the human tongue. He looked to Esha. "What was that one?"

"Belanorise," she answered without thought.

He nodded. "I like the Rannoran better. It flows nicer and is easier on the ears."

To her surprise, Esha found herself fighting a smile.

Kendrick returned his attention to Savita. "I understand your hesitation. I'd do the same in your shoes."

"You speak as if you're used to being in charge," Savita stated.

He shrugged. "You could say that. I want nothing from the elves other than to join forces and look for this adversary we're both hunting. It's attacked your people and mine. There may be things you know that I doona or vice versa."

"And if we agree?" Savita asked skeptically.

Kendrick's gaze briefly slid to Esha. "Then we work together. I can sleep somewhere separate. You never have to show me your location. Though I hope we'll become allies in the end. Trust has to be earned. It can no' be given."

"I suppose I already know your thoughts," Savita said to Esha.

Esha regarded Kendrick for a moment before she met her sister's gaze. "I wouldn't have brought him this far if I didn't agree with his sentiment."

Savita turned and walked a few paces closer to the waterfall. Esha found her gaze drawn back to Kendrick. He was watching her. She felt his gaze on her so many times, but it didn't unnerve her as she expected. He seemed to be intrigued by her just as much as she was with him.

Savita turned on her heel and walked back to them. She halted in front of Kendrick. "We can't abide lies. You claim—"

"I doona *claim* anything. I speak the truth," he replied bluntly, his tone clipped with the barest hint of anger.

Savita's eyes blazed with ire. "No one interrupts me."

"Then stop alluding to me being a liar. As I told Esha, I believed elves were a myth before today. There are things out there you may no' believe in, but they are verra real."

"Like your *assertion* that you're a dragon?" Savita fired back.

The tension was growing higher. Esha glanced at the Rangers around her. They were too far away to hear the conversation, but they seemed to sense the change between Kendrick and Savita.

"You want to see the truth? Fine," Kendrick said and turned to stalk away.

Esha started after him, even as she told herself not to.

Kendrick suddenly whirled back to face them. He raised his voice as he said, "Doona say I didna warn you."

With that, he was gone, replaced by an enormous dragon. Esha gasped, her gaze traveling up and up and up until she met the beast's sapphire eyes. She took a half-step back before she could stop herself. Her breathing was loud, even to her ears. She hadn't remembered drawing her sword, but it was in her hands.

The dragon did nothing. It simply stood there, watching them. Esha had seen Kendrick change into the dragon, but her brain had difficulty processing the truth of it. Shifters weren't real. Yet one stood before her now.

She gazed at the dragon as her curiosity pushed past the fear. Deep reddish-brown scales the color of sienna glistened with a metallic sheen in the sun. The scales were narrow over his body, growing into thick plates down his spine. The ones on Kendrick's belly were curved and a shade or two lighter than the rest of him.

Her gaze returned to his head. It was angular, with two twisting horns that curved slightly outward. She spotted two teeth poking from either side of his mouth, sending another spiral of fear through her. Then she remembered that he could've killed her at any time. But he hadn't. She returned to her perusal and followed the scales down his long, barbed tail. Then to his four limbs and the incredibly long talons. His wings were folded against him, but she wanted to see them.

"Can I see your wings?" she asked.

Kendrick immediately unfurled them. Esha was taken aback by the sheer size of them, but they *would* have to be massive to let him fly.

In the next instant, he was back in human form. Esha couldn't find words as he walked to her and Savita. It was only then that she looked around at her squad. Everyone had drawn weapons. Some had surprise and fascination on their faces, but a few didn't hide their derision.

Esha swung her gaze back to Kendrick to find him standing before her, his hands clasped behind his back once more. She swallowed, a thousand questions tumbling through her head.

"Can all dragons shift?" Savita asked.

Kendrick slid his gaze to her. "Nay."

"What makes you different?"

"I'm a Dragon King."

Esha heard the words and knew they fit him to perfection. How could she know that? She'd just met Kendrick. Had she somehow known deep within her subconscious that he was different? Was that why she wanted him to meet Savita? Was that why she'd considered working with him to hunt the entity?

She couldn't answer those questions, though she knew Savita would ask her the same things later.

"I'll leave now and never return if you ask it," Kendrick said. "However, I think it beneficial for our two societies to work together. If I stay, I'll share about the dragons and the Kings and hope you will impart the same about your culture."

Savita swallowed as she contemplated his offer. "Things might have gone a lot different if you had shown Esha your other form earlier."

"That's my true form," Kendrick explained.

A dragon. There was a real dragon standing before her, one that could shapeshift. Esha could hardly believe it. Her heart had yet to stop racing. It would be ridiculous to turn him away. He could very well have as much magic as the elves, which could only help in stopping their shared foe.

"Yes," Esha said. "We accept."

"Esha!" Savita snapped.

She turned to her sister. "You know it's the right call."

"I've not consulted the runes."

"Read them then. But you'll get the same answer."

Savita's eyes narrowed as she glared. Her voice lowered to the barest whisper as she said, "You're overstepping, *Ranger*."

"I know my position. And yours. I'm not questioning or challenging you. You've not fought that thing. You have not seen how easily it took down the Rangers. And an alliance is always a good step."

Savita's nostrils flared, though she kept her expression passive. She directed her words to Kendrick but never took her eyes off Esha. "We will track with you, but you will remain far from us. You'll not be allowed entry to Flamefall under any circumstances."

"I accept," Kendrick said.

"As for you," she said to Esha as she took a step closer, "we'll discuss this later. In private." Savita turned on her heel and stalked away.

Esha blew out a breath and motioned for Kendrick to follow. She hated arguing with her sister, and Esha usually went out of her way to prevent such altercations. But this time was different. She felt it in her bones. Though she probably shouldn't have spoken before Savita read the runes.

"There's tension there," Kendrick said as he caught up with her.

She shrugged. "Siblings fight. Didn't you bicker with yours?"

"I didn't have any brothers or sisters."

Was it her imagination, or did she hear a note of longing in his voice? She was already feeling too much when it came to the Dragon King. Perhaps she should have someone else track with him. Then she considered everything he could share about his world, and she quickly forgot that inane thought.

She sheathed her sword and looked ahead. In the next heartbeat, she glanced back at him. He was a shapeshifter. A real dragon. A Dragon *King*.

Chapter Five

The atmosphere had shifted. Kendrick couldn't deny it if he tried. Before, the elves had been wary of him, but now, a few projected...maybe not open hostility, but something close to it.

Then there was Esha.

Without a doubt, she had been excited to see him in his true form—after her initial surge of fear. The elves had never seen a dragon before, much less one that shifted. He imagined it had been something of a surprise. But the way Esha's eyes glowed had quickened his blood. It had taken all his control to look away from her and fight the intense wave of desire that enveloped him.

The sisters had tried to keep their voices lowered, but his enhanced hearing had picked up every word of their conversation. Savita's anger toward Esha worried him. Savita had been leaning toward agreeing to his terms, but Esha's words had undercut Savita's command. How that would affect him in the long run was anyone's guess, but he wouldn't turn his back on Savita anytime soon. If the way the others treated her was any indication, she wielded tremendous power—and he wasn't keen on finding out just how much.

"They'll get over their shock and fear soon," Esha said as if reading his mind. "They weren't expecting to see you shift."

"Neither were you."

She kept her gaze straight ahead. "You did warn me."

"Need I remind you that you didna believe me?"

A ghost of a smile played on her full lips. "You'll understand, of course, why."

"Of course. After all, there are no elves where I come from."

Her golden eyes briefly met his. "You could've killed us at any moment."

"Note that I didna."

This time, she chuckled. "It is noted, Dragon King. We Rangers have patrolled the plateau and surrounding areas for generations. We believed we knew every creature and danger out there."

"I've recently learned that there is always something new to discover. It can be good. Oftentimes, it isna."

"No truer words have been spoken," she said softly.

Kendrick looked ahead to where Savita walked at the front of the group of Rangers. "What is your sister's role, exactly?"

"All elves are born with magic. It's innate in each of us, but a special few have an additional ability. Savita is one of those rare few who can read the rune stones."

"Rune stones?" he asked with a frown, thinking of the stones the Norse used.

Esha nodded, causing the chain on her ear to swing. "When a decision needs to be made, the Readers turn to the runes. The stones only communicate with those like Savita."

"So no' just anyone can learn?"

"Anyone can *learn*, but it's pointless if the runes don't respond."

So it wasn't like tarot, either. "Do you mean to say the stones actually *talk* to Savita?"

"That's how she describes it. They don't have a conversation like this, but it is a back and forth."

"We have similar things. The difference is, anyone can learn to read and decipher them."

"You would trust just anyone with your decisions?" she asked, dismay in her gaze.

"We doona use those tools as you do."

"But you have them?"

"Something similar, aye."

"How...unusual." She wore a frown as she looked forward once again.

Kendrick waited for her to continue. When she didn't, he gave her a nudge. "I gather your sister is important?"

"Those who have the abilities of a Reader are revered."

"Which puts them in a position of power."

Esha cut her gaze to him for a heartbeat. "Of course, it does. We might all have magic, but critical decisions, judgments, and resolutions are left to the runes and those who can read them. Always."

Kendrick didn't point out again that Esha had taken that from Savita. The more he thought about it, the more he knew that only trouble would come from that action. "How did you and Savita end up together? Or is it normal for families to be stationed together?"

"It isn't," Esha said after a brief pause. "She was stationed elsewhere when I began my training. Unlike Readers, anyone can become a Ranger if they show enough skill and dedication. It's a difficult way of life, but we pledge ourselves to it."

He got an uneasy feeling about what pledging meant. He suspected he knew, but he would wait to ask. For now, he wanted to know more about Savita. He assumed his biggest opposition would come from there. "In other words, you two were apart for some time?"

"We were. I never expected to see her again. Apparently, the runes told her she was needed here. Savita left Belanore, where she'd been in service, and came here."

Kendrick glanced at Esha and took a gamble. "I imagine it was nice to see your sister again."

"Yes."

That one word, tightly said, spoke volumes.

Kendrick looked at the wall of earth that rose sharply before him. He had yet to see a way to get to the top of the plateau. He spotted Savita and saw that she climbed camouflaged stairs in the side. The steps switchbacked all the way to the summit, which was a considerable ascent.

"Did you think we got up another way?" Esha asked, a note of laughter in her voice.

He glanced at her and grinned. "I could get us to the top faster."

"I bet you could."

Kendrick stared into her beautiful eyes as something passed between them. It was lust, pure and simple. It wasn't the first time he had felt such desire, but it had been a long while. And his body responded instantly.

Esha looked away first. She moved in front of him and began to ascend. Kendrick glanced upward, his eyes landing on her perfectly formed bottom. His body reacted with an instant flash of desire so intense it stole his breath. He forced himself to look away from the appealing woman who captured his attention like no other before placing his foot on the first stair. He was here to learn about the elves and hunt the entity, not to seduce a particularly beautiful and bewitching elf. Which was too bad because he suspected they would be good together.

There was no conversation as they made their way to the top. He often glanced toward the border, his gaze taking in the scenery. He needed to contact Con. He planned on doing it as soon as he was settled for the night. In the meantime, he wanted to gather more information to relay.

It took a significant amount of time to reach the top of the plateau. When they did, Esha paused to wait for him. Kendrick first noted the heat and humidity. It hung so thick in the air he could almost cut it. Then he took in the lush plateau. Before him sat a tropical rainforest biome with all its beauty, the entire area overflowing with plants. The thick, soaring canopy of trees beckoned him to explore, and the sounds of the animals called him to investigate.

"Rannora is to the south," Esha said and pointed to the right.

Kendrick followed her finger but didn't see a city, only more thick, tangled jungle. "Tell me more," he urged.

"The Ever Reaching River cuts through the plateau, dissecting it," she answered.

"I can no' wait to see it."

"Belanore is across the river to the northwest. There are smaller settlements elsewhere, but most choose the cities. It's safer that way."

He looked at her. "Safer from what?"

"Our land might be beautiful, but beasts like the taste of us and often try to have us for a meal."

"Thanks for the heads-up."

She grinned. "I doubt you have anything to worry about."

"I've found there is always someone stronger—and always someone weaker."

"Then I should warn you about the Dark Elves."

Finally, something about the elves. "Why is that?"

"They aren't known for making friends."

If there were Dark, then there had to be Light. Were they classified as such like the Fae? "I take it you're a Light Elf?"

She chuckled. "Not exactly."

Kendrick noted that Savita and the Rangers led the way through the thick rainforest, heading north. They walked as if there were a trail, but Kendrick didn't see any indication of that. He scanned the massive trees, taking in the thick vines hanging from the limbs high above him and cataloging the different sounds of animals. Suddenly, Esha turned them to the south.

They walked a few minutes before she said, "I'm a Sun Elf. Sometimes, we're called Gold Elves or even Desert Elves because of our coloring."

"And the markings on your face?"

She lifted a shoulder. "It's a personal preference. Some have more than others, but yes, most do have markings somewhere on their bodies."

"And the Dark Elves?"

"There are seven classes of elves. Sun, Moon, Star, Sea, Wood, Mountain, and Dark. We prefer certain places, as you can probably guess by some of the names."

"In other words, Mountain Elves will be in the mountains?"

Esha's lips curved into a grin. "Exactly. Though, as I'm sure you noticed, the Rangers are made up of all different classes."

"Even the Dark? I assume by the name that they're evil."

"Are all your kind good?"

He shook his head.

"Are they all evil?"

Kendrick chuckled. "I get your point."

"Dark Elves are called that because they live underground. That changed their appearance. You'll recognize them by their gray skin and eyes that can be yellow or gray. Their hair is usually white. They're known for their proud disposition. They also don't understand or agree with mercy of any kind. Many call them cruel and brutal, but some say it is just the strict code they live by."

"Do the Dark Elves interact with others?"

"They do, but everyone who encounters them should be aware of who they're dealing with."

"And the Sun Elves?"

She picked her way through the dense underbrush and kept her heading. "We're known for our levelheadedness. That isn't to say we don't do rash things on occasion, but we usually think things through."

Kendrick could see that. He briefly thought of Savita. What he had seen so far told him she liked the power her position gave her. And she didn't like being undermined in any way. "What about your idea of mercy?"

"You're here, aren't you?" she replied with a smile.

"That I am."

"Sun Elves have more Readers than any other class—though that isn't to say our magic is greater or better. However, I will admit that others say we like to *believe* our magic is greater."

"It could just mean the runes like Sun Elves."

She laughed softly.

Kendrick looked over his shoulder. He wondered where Savita and the Rangers had gone. He slid his gaze back to Esha. "As I said, trust has to be earned, but I want you to know that I'm here as a friend. I have no desire to betray you in any way."

"I hope you hold to that." Esha pushed aside a thick plant and walked past it. Then she halted and faced him. "We might know very little about dragons, especially Dragon Kings, but that doesn't mean we fear you. You could have stronger magic. You might even be able to take over our land—"

"I willna do any of that."

"What I'm saying is that you can try, but there are more of us than you know. We *would* get our land back."

He applauded her fierceness. She might appear at ease as they spoke, but he had yet to gain her trust. That went both ways, though. It was why he kept looking over his shoulder. The Rangers were out there, watching him. Just as the Kings would watch anyone on their land.

Instead of replying, Kendrick looked over her shoulder to see a decent-sized rocky shoreline and water. He walked past her and noted that it was a large lake. "This is stunning. I take it I'll be staying here?"

"You will. There's one more thing. We would appreciate it if you remained in this form."

He met her gaze. "You doona want others to know a dragon is here."

"Precisely."

Kendrick studied the shoreline and found the perfect place for his tent. He thought of the yurt V had built for Claire during Valentine's Day. The Kings, as a rule, didn't rely heavily on their magic if they could avoid it, but this was a different scenario. So, Kendrick didn't hesitate and used his magic to craft a yurt of his own. Then he sat back and grinned. When he glanced at Esha, the Ranger's mouth was slack with surprise.

"That's what your magic can do?"

"Aye. Want to see inside?" He held open the flap and waited.

Chapter Six

As if Esha would refuse to see what kind of structure a Dragon King's magic could create. She ducked her head and entered the rounded shelter. It was about the size of her tent in Flamefall, but the inside was much different.

A single pole about as thick as Kendrick's leg stood in the middle of the tent, holding up everything. Tiny lights hung from the pole, extending outward and around the tent's perimeter. Thick rugs with beautiful designs and colors covered the floor. The bed was large and off to one side. Across from that was a square table, sitting low to the ground. On either side of it were plush pillows in various colors. Additional scattered cushions offered more seating.

"Amazing," she whispered. She turned to Kendrick, who had stopped beside her inside. "How did you do this?"

He shrugged. "I thought of it."

"Just thought of it?"

"Aye."

That was much stronger magic than any elf could do. It gave her pause because if he could do this kind of magic and couldn't find the entity they sought, how would the elves ever manage it? More than that, she realized just how easily the dragons could wipe out the elves.

"The fear I saw when I shifted didna last long. I hope this doesna either."

She couldn't meet his gaze. "I suppose that demonstrates how little we know of dragons."

"We're sharing information, right? You tell me about the elves, and I tell you about dragons."

Esha nodded slowly. That was part of the deal. She had never felt so off-balance before. A formidable being stood beside her, but if he hadn't shown her his magic, she wouldn't have any idea of his power. She met his gaze and stared into his green eyes. Even as her mind cautioned her to tread carefully, she didn't regret anything that had happened since she'd come across Kendrick. Nor did she want to be anywhere but where she was right now.

With a mighty Dragon King who offered knowledge of his people.

This was the start of something. Esha felt it in the depths of her being. The possibilities were endless. And she was in the midst of it all.

Kendrick's lips curved into a smile. She tried not to notice how his eyes sparkled and her mouth tipped up in answer. All of a sudden, she became aware that they were alone. And standing close together. Her gaze lowered to his shoulders and lingered. The thin material of his shirt outlined the definition of each muscle.

Her thoughts veered into dangerous territory. He was a guest, a potential ally. She shouldn't be contemplating what he looked like with his shirt removed. Or what it might be like to run her hands over his warm skin.

To be held tightly against his hard body.

Warmth spread through her as her mouth went dry. Esha blinked and drew in a shaky breath. She lifted her gaze to find Kendrick watching her raptly. Embarrassment washed over her. She hadn't felt that emotion since she was a young girl. All she could do was hope that he didn't realize where her thoughts had gone.

Their gazes held for several heartbeats. Then he asked, "Would you like some tea?"

"You drink our tea?"

"If you explain it, I can make some. However, I was going to brew some of mine."

"I'd like to try yours."

"Does that mean you can stay for a wee bit?"

Esha hesitated. On the one hand, she very much wanted to stay with Kendrick and learn about him. On the other, she knew she had to face Savita sooner or later. Maybe giving her sister some time to consider things would calm her anger.

It was an excuse. One Esha fully admitted to herself because she didn't want to leave Kendrick. "For a little while, yes."

The delight on his face made her stomach flutter unexpectedly. She parted her lips, attempting to drag more air into her lungs. He motioned for her to choose a seat. She moved to the low table and arranged the brightly colored pillows around her. They were lush and extremely comfortable. When she looked up, Kendrick was headed her way with a tray that held a teapot, three smaller containers, and two cups.

He set it on the table. "Where I'm from, we drink copious amounts of tea. Sometimes, we put honey, sugar, or milk in it. There are even those who put lemon." He flashed her a smile as he lowered himself to the pillows. "This is my favorite tea."

"What is it called?"

"Earl Grey. It's a black tea."

He poured a cup and handed it to her. Esha sniffed the liquid, liking the smell. Then she watched as he added a bit of honey to his, stirred, and took a sip. He grinned and waited for her to taste it.

Esha brought the cup to her lips and sipped. It wasn't bad, but it wasn't the kind of tea she was used to. She added honey and tried again. Better, but not quite. She then added milk and grinned at the result.

"It's good," she said.

Kendrick laughed, causing the corners of his eyes to crease. "We'll try yours next. Will you finish telling me about the classes of elves?"

She had expected the question. Esha held the cup between her hands and settled herself more comfortably as she drank. "Let's see. I told you about the Sun and Dark Elves. There are also the Moon Elves. They don't like to mingle with others and are very reclusive. Their skin is very fair with a silver glow to it. Their hair ranges from black, blue, to silvery-white, and their eyes are commonly various shades of blue. You won't see them, simply because they cannot abide being around the rest of us."

Kendrick leaned one elbow on a pillow as he drank. "Was it because of a war?"

"Nothing like that. What you need to understand is that elves are amiable at the core, but if you put us together, you start to see the variations and how dramatic each class can be. The Moon Elves *will* show themselves, but they'd rather not. We had one as a Ranger long ago, but none since."

"That makes me want to see if I can find a Moon Elf."

She laughed because she knew he was being serious. "That brings me to the Star Elves. They also have light skin. Many will mistake them for Moon Elves because of that. However, Star Elves have hair of lavender, purple, or silver and all have various shades of purple eyes. They're nomadic, preferring to move rather than stay in one place. That means you'll encounter many Star Elves because they love to meet others. They're curious and adventurous, though they can be focused and relentless at times. They're amazing healers."

Kendrick nodded, his gaze locked on her as he took another drink. "Fascinating. Continue, please."

Esha couldn't remember the last time someone had listened so raptly to what she had to say. It was exciting and frightening all at once. Mostly because of how good it made her feel. "Sea Elves. Their skin has a blue or greenish tint. I love their hair. It ranges from a bluish-black to greenish-black. Their eyes are normally iridescent blue to silvery-white. They have webbed fingers and toes, as well as gills behind their ears."

"I take it they live in the water?"

"They can, and do, come on land. But, yes, they prefer bodies of water for their homes."

Kendrick frowned briefly. "We have something like that. A myth, really. They're called mermaids or mermen. Their top halves are human, and their bottom halves have fish tails."

"Really?" Esha asked, trying to form an image of such a creature in her mind. "Maybe it's a good thing they're a myth."

He laughed.

"That brings us to the Wood Elves. They are the guardians of all things in the forest. They live in harmony with it in a way I've always found calming. They're good with animals, and they can sense truths and lies. They can be judgmental but take time to consider everything before passing judgment. A Wood Elf's friendship, once won, is deep and lasting. They're expert fighters—some of the best, really. You'll know them by their coppery skin. Their hair is mostly brown to red, and their eyes are always green or hazel."

"Which leaves us with the Mountain Elves."

"Ah, yes," she said and paused to drink. The tea was growing on her. "They're not as isolated as the Moon or Dark Elves, but they make their homes in the mountains, and that keeps them more separate than any other classes. They are the rarest of all the elves. They're cautious and aloof by nature and understand the importance of community. They're shorter in stature with black or brown hair. Their skin can range from white for those who live in the colder regions to more of a brown tint in other areas. Their eyes are always black, and they are the finest weapons crafters among us."

Kendrick finished his tea and sat up to pour another cup. "I saw Wood, Sea, Star, and Sun Elves in your unit of Rangers. You all work together well."

"The Rangers are a way of life. It isn't something agreed to in the spur of the moment. When I decided I wanted to be a Ranger, I was tested. Repeatedly. Not just with weapons but also with my mind, wit, and emotions. Our duty is to keep travelers safe, but also to halt any trouble we might find along the way. Being an Asavori Ranger means that you have passed countless tests, trained with the best fighters, learned strategy, and are able to put—and use—all that together."

Kendrick's green eyes held hers. "Sounds intense."

"It took years."

"That brings me to my next question. What is the lifespan of an elf?"

She grinned. "Much, much longer than a mortal. We live for centuries, sometimes reaching even a thousand years old. What about dragons?"

"They live for thousands of years."

Her smile tightened at his words. "And a Dragon King?"

Kendrick slowly leaned to the side, resting on his elbow once more. "I'm no' sure you want to know that."

"I do." She did, didn't she?

He glanced at the ground and said, "It's a little complicated. A Dragon King lives until the magic deems someone more worthy should take his place."

"How old are you?"

A flash of something swept over his face. "I have lived so long I no longer remember the number."

With that, he set down his cup and rose, walking to the side of the tent, his back to her. Esha watched him for a beat before placing her cup down and getting to her feet. Something had changed. The atmosphere was no longer friendly and open. She saw a strain in him now, and she wished she could undo it.

"That was an insensitive question," she said.

He blew out a breath and turned to her. "Nay, lass. You have every right to ask. It just made me think of the past. At times, it feels like a wave of desolation will take me if I think too hard about it. Sometimes, I'm unable to fight it off. The depression is…daunting and verra difficult to shake. I usually take to my mountain and sleep when I sense it coming."

"Then I will leave you to rest."

He reached out and gently grabbed her arm, halting her, his face lined with remorse. "I meant dragon sleep. Where we sleep for centuries. It's how I've gotten through so many endless years."

Blood rushed through Esha's ears as his words registered. Just how old *was* he? By his words, exceptionally old. But he didn't look it. Surely, he wasn't immortal. Or was he?

He released her arm. "Please, doona go. I've been patrolling my area for weeks on my own. One of my brethren disappeared recently, and it brought up a lot of things I've been ignoring. I want to learn about your people, and I want to work with you to hunt that thing I fought."

Esha had been with him for long enough. She should return to Flamefall and speak to Savita. She knew it. Instead, she said, "Tell me about your people."

His smile was slow and nearly blinding. "Dragons are amazing. They come in every size and color you could think of. Some might say we're righteous creatures, and they wouldna be wrong. As you said earlier, however, there are always good, bad, and everything in between. Magic looks deep inside each dragon to find the strongest—the most powerful of each clan. The magic chose me to be a King."

She grinned at the light that shone in his eyes when he spoke about the dragons.

"Each clan is a different color. Mine is sienna. The previous King was gravely wounded in battle, leaving us weakened and vulnerable." Kendrick's smile faded as he lowered himself back onto the cushions. He was silent for a moment as he poured more tea into both his cup and hers. As he added honey, he said, "Only a Dragon King can kill another King. That's how one becomes a King."

Her stomach twisted. She returned to the pillows and wrapped her hands around her cup. "You had to…kill him?"

"It was a mercy in the end. We heal quickly, but he had battled another King, and the damage he sustained was extensive. He was a good King—one of the best. When I came to take his place, he smiled. I'll never forget that. He knew I would give him the end he desired so the pain would stop."

"But you carry that around."

"Every King does." He shot her a half smile. "It is our way."

She swallowed, her mind latching on to something he'd said. "Wait. If only a King can kill another King, then I take it you all fight often to take each other's spots?"

"No' at all. As I said, the magic decides who should be King. Anyone can challenge us, but it is always to the death. Someone will die. Many want to be King but doona get the magic's call. That ultimately leads to their death. The other Dragon Kings are my brethren. We lean on each other for everything."

Esha's heart slammed into her ribs with shock as her mind connected everything. "If you can only die by another Dragon King's hand, and none of you fights, then that would make you..."

"Immortal," he replied in a soft voice.

"Oh." What exactly did she say to that? What *could* she say?

Immortal. What was that even like? She wanted to ask, but his words from before stopped her. Obviously, it wasn't all it seemed. The despondency she had seen in his eyes earlier told of the things he carried inside him—things she could only imagine.

"Does that change things between us?" Kendrick asked.

She looked into his eyes and shook her head. "No."

His answering grin was all she needed.

Chapter Seven

Esha seemed hard to surprise. Kendrick had clearly shaken her with his admission but not enough to frighten her away. That pleased him. Probably more than it should if he were being honest.

He watched as her gaze moved to the entry. He knew she was about to leave and found that he didn't want her to go. He had more things to learn. Then there was the fact that he liked her company. A lot. She seemed curious about him, too—or, at least, interested to learn about the Dragon Kings. But that didn't bother him. He was just as fascinated with the elves.

His thoughts drifted to the problems Cullen and Shaw had dealt with at Stonemore. The human city abhorred anything involving magic and based their religion around annihilating it. Kendrick wondered how the people of Stonemore would feel about facing elves. After all, those humans had systematically wiped out the villages and cities near them, slaughtering those with magic along the way.

Stonemore wasn't the only place where mortals feared those with magic. Yet every human who spurned someone for being different put those with magic on the run, fighting for their lives and hiding in fear.

Perhaps those with magic could find a home with the elves. It was something Kendrick would discuss with Esha later. If things worked out between their people and they became allies, perhaps they might join the dragons if there were a war with the humans—though he really didn't want more bloodshed. He'd seen enough of that for eternity.

"What is it?" Esha asked.

Kendrick started to tell her that it was nothing, then reconsidered. "You said there are humans in Shecrish."

"There are."

"And some have magic."

"Some do, aye."

"Would your people accept other humans? Particularly those with magic?"

Esha's brow puckered. "Why?"

"I can go into detail later, but suffice it to say they're finding it difficult to live where they are now."

She seemed to think for a moment before shrugging. "I'm not saying that humans *don't* find their way to us—there are those who wander. However, most of the mortals here arrived as infants and simply chose to remain."

That brought up another question. It seemed every being on this planet arrived as an infant. So far, no one knew who brought them or how they got here. "Do you know how the bairns get to Zora?"

"Bairns?" she asked with a frown.

"Babies," he explained.

Esha shook her head. "I was going to ask if the dragons were responsible."

"Nay, lass, we're no'." He took a breath, deciding on the next question. "You said earlier that you bring elves here who arrive in other places on the realm. How?"

"Magic, of course. It takes a lot of it, and it's not something that just anyone can do. We have Callers who gather every month and link their magic."

"Do the Callers bring elves every time?"

"Yes. Most times, it's just one, but there have been a few times where there were two. Never more than that."

"Because the Callers' magic isna strong enough?"

"It's been assumed that it was because only those were out there at the time. But now that you mention it, I can't say that for certain."

Kendrick nodded, taking that in. He started to open his mouth for another question, but she spoke first.

"I need to see my sister. The longer I put it off, the worse things will be," Esha said as she got to her feet.

He reluctantly stood, feeling strangely out of sorts that she was leaving. "Of course."

"I'll be back. You've told me very little about the dragons."

Kendrick grinned. "I promise to tell you more when you return."

"Good."

She stood there, staring at him. The golden-amber hue of her eyes ensnared him. Everything about her fascinated him. A million questions buzzed through his mind, but he kept coming back to wanting to know *her*. What had her life been like? Who had raised her? And what had occurred to make her join the Rangers?

"This area isn't heavily traveled. You shouldn't have any visitors," Esha said.

"I'm no' worried."

"No, I don't suppose you would be. Does anything frighten you?"

Another war with humans. But he didn't say that. "Everyone is scared of something."

"Even you?"

"Even me," he admitted.

Esha turned her head, causing the chain on her ear to sway. "We'll speak soon, Dragon King."

"Good luck with your sister, Sun Elf."

She grinned and turned on her heel to walk out of the yurt. Kendrick followed and watched as she broke into a run. It wasn't long before she vanished into the forest. She was quick—something else he filed away about the elves. Was that just something a Sun Elf could do? Or was that all elves? It was another question he'd have to ask her.

Kendrick glanced at the sky. The day had progressed faster than he'd realized. The sun was already on its descent. He sighed and decided to explore the area. He walked the edge of the lake on one side, noting that it was much larger than he'd first realized.

He retraced his steps to the yurt. The rocks along the water were different in size, the stones smooth and brightly colored in an assortment of hues that glistened in the fading daylight. He walked in increasingly larger circles around the yurt, studying the ground for any tracks—be they human or animal.

Kendrick found some that resembled a deer and more that could be something like a fox, but until he saw the animals and learned what they were, he couldn't say for sure. The lake was large enough that animals had a variety of locations from which to drink, so he wasn't worried about encountering anything.

Once he was satisfied with his search, he took a walk on the other side of the lake. When the sun was about to set, he made his way back to his camp, gathering firewood along the way. He started a fire and sat before it, watching the sky darken over the shimmering water. He thought about the day, arranging his thoughts. When he next focused, the sky was black.

Kendrick had put it off long enough. It was time to contact Con. Just as he opened the mental link to say Con's name, he saw movement off to the side. He couldn't see anything, even with his superior eyesight, which alerted him that magic was being used. It didn't feel like the entity—there wasn't a shimmer or anything.

But he knew someone was there.

"It's rude to stare," Kendrick stated. "Join me or leave."

Shadows moved and shifted, and then a Dark Elf walked out. He stood tall, his yellow eyes locked on Kendrick. The elf wore a long, black coat, the bottom cut into six thick strips. The shoulders had armor plating. Beneath the jacket, the elf wore a shirt with chest and abdomen armor. Black trousers were tucked into knee-high boots with armor on the fronts. Kendrick saw no weapons, but that didn't mean there weren't any.

He looked at the elf's face. He had pulled the top part of his long, white hair away from his face, exposing pointed ears. His gray skin showed thick, white brows that slashed over yellow eyes. There were multiple scars on his face. The deepest ran from the inside corner of his left eye and cut diagonally down his left cheek to his jaw. Another bisected his mouth at an angle right to left. A third ran from his left temple through his left brow, then across his nose and along the right cheek.

The elf walked to the opposite side of the fire and elegantly sank to the ground. Kendrick noted the small, silver metal bands around locks of his hair. Two on one side, one on the other.

"I didn't imagine you to be so amenable, Dragon King," the elf stated.

Kendrick quirked a brow. "Word travels fast."

"Did you imagine it wouldn't?"

"I doona think it matters either way."

The elf snorted. "That just proves you know nothing of elves or Shecrish."

"That's something I plan to rectify." Kendrick shifted. "Let's start with names. I'm Kendrick."

Yellow eyes watched him for a long moment. "Dain."

"Your entry was interesting. What can I do for you?"

"It's what I can do for you."

Kendrick grinned. "Is that so?"

Dain leaned on one hand and propped a foot on the ground, his knee bent. "It is."

"Why?"

"You'll disregard me if I tell you. It's better if you find out for yourself."

Kendrick mimicked the elf's posture. "Or you could just tell me."

"What would be the fun in that?"

Kendrick hated to admit it, but he liked Dain. The Dark Elf had come for a reason, and it wasn't just to spar with words—though Kendrick enjoyed it. The warning was real, and he suspected that Dain wouldn't tell him anything more, no matter how much he pushed.

Dain's gaze was steady as he held Kendrick's. "Dark Elves are feared."

"Is it warranted?"

"Sometimes," he admitted.

Kendrick nodded. "The same could be said for the Kings."

"Then you understand."

Kendrick did, in fact. Those terrified of the Dragon Kings usually had no reason other than they were told to be. They knew nothing about dragons. Esha had told Kendrick that the Dark Elves could be cruel and never showed mercy. That didn't mean they were evil. It was simply their way.

"Tell me what brought you here," Kendrick asked as he sat up.

Dain turned his head slightly and lowered his gaze to the ground. "Another time." The elf rose to his feet in one fluid motion. "One word of caution. Not everything is as it seems."

In the next instant, shadows flowed around him, covering Dain completely. Then they vanished, taking the elf with them.

Kendrick didn't have time to think about that before he heard someone approaching. His dragon eyes probed the dark jungle, and he hoped it was Esha. Instead, Savita made her way to him. She didn't stop until she stood in the same place Dain had been.

"May I join you?" Savita asked.

Kendrick held out his hand, his palm up as he motioned for her to sit. "Of course."

He thought Savita might balk at sitting on the ground, but she said nothing as she lowered herself. She watched him over the dancing flames, her copper eyes giving nothing away. Savita hadn't come just to soak in the moonlight. She was here for a reason, but Kendrick didn't intend to say anything until she announced her intention.

The silence grew, broken only by the pop of the fire and the gently lapping waves of the water on the shore. If the elf thought she could make him nervous or apprehensive, she was about to learn that it would take much more.

"I want your word that you will leave in three days."

He had expected a time limit to his stay, but not one so soon. "You think we can find this entity and kill it in three days?"

"Is that too much for you?"

"What is it you doona like about me?" he pressed.

She lifted one shoulder. "I don't trust you."

"Nor I you. But that's what I want to do. Build trust."

"The runes have spoken."

He didn't completely disregard the runes or the idea that they could speak to the Readers, but he felt as if Savita were using them as an excuse to get rid of him. Though only she would know since she was the only one who could read them. "What did they say?"

"You bring death."

"The thing I'm tracking is what brought it to your lands, no' me."

She tilted her head to the side. "We've faced many dangers in Shecrish, but nothing like this. The runes told me it was something new. Something that came about at your arrival."

Kendrick's stomach churned. He had feared such a thing and wasn't the only one, but he had held out hope that this new foe had been here all along. "Excuse me?"

"You aren't of our world."

Shite. Maybe the runes *did* speak to her. There was no other way she could know that information.

"Nay."

"Go home. The entity will leave us alone if you do."

He frowned and shook his head. "You can no' be certain of that."

"The runes do not lie," she stated, a hint of anger in her words.

Kendrick tried to think of something to say when Savita rose.

She looked down at him. "Leave. Or more blood will cover you."

He watched her leave, her words echoing in his head.

Chapter Eight

Esha fought the anger rising like a storm as she caught sight of Savita just outside Flamefall. When Esha arrived to speak to her sister, she was told she had to wait. She kept herself busy until she tried to see Savita again, only to be told that her sister was busy. After more waiting, Esha tried a third time. That's when she learned that Savita had gone to see Kendrick.

Savita stopped before her now, her eyes cold and angry. "You know I make the decisions."

Esha remained silent, even though a retort lay heavy upon her lips.

"Don't ever undermine me again," Savita stated in a low voice. "We might have been raised together, but that won't save you from punishment."

Savita had always liked to be in control and make the decisions. Even when they were young. Nothing had changed other than the power her sister now held. Savita had a gift, but sometimes it was hard to take. Especially when Savita lorded it over Esha as she did now.

"I was right, wasn't I?" Esha asked. "The runes said Kendrick was an ally, didn't they?"

Her sister held her gaze for a long moment. "The threat to us hasn't changed."

Esha blinked and took a step back. "You can't honestly think Kendrick is the threat the runes spoke of. That's the thing we're tracking. The creature that kills our people. Kendrick could be our friend. Do you have any idea what kind of magic he wields?"

"I know."

"He told you, then? He's not trying to hide anything."

"Everyone hides something, sister."

Esha shook her head. "Not everyone. I don't."

"Don't you?"

The softly spoken question made Esha's heart jump into her throat. If Savita asked the runes the right questions, then she would know Esha's deepest thoughts about Kendrick.

"He's leaving in three days."

"What?" No. That couldn't be. That wasn't enough time to defeat the foe. Esha and her squad had been tracking it for over a month and had found nothing.

Savita shrugged and walked around her. "That's all the time he has."

"Did he tell you that? Or did you tell *him*?" Esha asked as she turned to stare after her sister.

Savita halted, then slowly turned to face Esha. "You question me?"

"It's a simple query. Did the runes tell you that timeframe?"

"Is it so shocking to think he might have to return to his people? It isn't as if he can remain here forever."

Esha realized that her sister hadn't answered the question. Savita only did that when she wanted to hide something and yet not lie outright. Which meant the runes hadn't told her to send Kendrick away. Why was her sister doing this? But then she knew. Esha had undermined Savita in front of others, and this was her sister's way of getting back at her.

It was childish and ridiculous. They had a way of gaining an ally, and no civilization was strong enough not to need friends. Not to mention that Kendrick's abilities, coupled with the Rangers', meant they had a better chance of finding and stopping their common enemy.

"Remember your place, sister," Savita said and walked away.

"Oh, I remember it," Esha whispered after her. "How could I ever forget?"

Esha took a deep breath and tried to curb the ire that ran rampant through her. She turned to go to Kendrick when she caught movement out of the corner of her eye. When she turned and looked in that direction, she saw nothing. Still, Esha remained in place, watching and waiting to see if it was the invisible enemy they were after. After a while, she began to think it was only her imagination.

She recalled how some of her Rangers had been wary of Kendrick. They didn't understand her interest in him, a shapeshifter. They also didn't know how much magic he wielded. Those were the same members who would eventually hunt with Kendrick on the morrow. Perhaps she needed to spend time with her team and convince them to give him a chance.

Esha looked toward Kendrick's camp before sighing and returning to

Flamefall. The Rangers' encampment had been constructed on the edge of the jungle. They'd chosen a section of earth that dipped to better keep their tents hidden. Guards were stationed all through the forest and the surrounding area that would alert them if anyone got close. Few ever did, simply because most people of Shecrish didn't venture far from the cities.

Esha nodded to other Rangers and eventually found her squad gathered outside their grouping of tents. They grew quiet as she approached. Esha stopped before them and let her gaze meet each of theirs.

"We're Rangers," she said. "We fight when it's needed, track when it's called for, and rescue when others can't. We gave up a softer life for this. Each of us has trained for decades. We've put our bodies and minds through torturous training to be given the title of Ranger. Not everyone who applies is accepted. Do we always agree with what we're sent to do? No, because we're rarely given details. But it doesn't matter. Right now, our directive is to hunt the thing that has killed our people." Esha paused and looked at the Wood Elf to her left. "Zentha, how long have we been attempting to track this adversary?"

Zentha swallowed and said, "Over a month."

Esha's gaze moved to Ryul. "Have we been successful?"

The Sun Elf shook his head of golden-blond hair. "We have not."

"Are we too proud to take assistance?" she demanded, her gaze moving around them.

A muscle worked in the jaw of the Wood Elf, Elduin. "We don't know him."

Elduin didn't need to explain who he was referring to. Esha knew. "And he doesn't know us. I'm not saying we should trust him right now, but we *will* be tracking with him starting tomorrow. We all saw him locked in battle today. He came out of it unscathed. Think about that. Then think about those we've lost when we tangled with our foe. I want the advantage, any advantage, that will allow us to put an end to any more of our people dying. I can't be the only one."

"You aren't," Zentha said.

Elduin shrugged. "You make some good points."

"I'd like to see what the Dragon King can do," Ryul added.

Esha grinned. "Me, too. Get some rest, Rangers. It's going to be a long day tomorrow."

At their nods and smiles, she turned away. Esha's gaze landed on Savita, who stood outside her tent, watching her. Normally, Esha would go to her sister and spend some time with her. But not tonight. Esha made her way to her tent and moved aside the flap as she entered. She straightened and looked around.

An image of Kendrick's round shelter filled her mind. It had been roomy, but so was hers. Her station gave her that benefit—unlike her squad, who had to bunk in pairs. Her eyes moved around her quarters. They had to be able to pack up and go at a moment's notice, but there were a few luxuries, like her bed. It wasn't the size of Kendrick's, but it was better than she used to have. The covers were soft and plush. The chairs were comfortable, and she even had a small table on which to eat her meals in private if she so chose. Then there was her favorite piece— the bath.

She unbuckled the straps that held her dagger at her thigh and placed it on the table. Next, she removed her sword. Esha pulled out a chair and sank heavily into it as she took off her boots and then her corset. She reclined in the chair and thought about how the Rangers lived.

They had always been told they could be moved at any time, but for as long as she had been with the Rangers, they hadn't relocated the camp even once. She wondered why they hadn't built better structures—not that they needed it, what they had sufficed. Though Savita's tent was twice the size of hers and held many more indulgences. But that was Savita.

Her sister had never understood Esha's desire to be a Ranger. Which was why it had been such a surprise when Savita had shown up at Flamefall. Esha loved her, and she appreciated having Savita there since so many others went years without seeing their families. But there were days, like today, that made Esha wish Savita were elsewhere.

No matter how far up the ranks Esha climbed, Savita would always make sure Esha remembered that she was the older sister and the one with more power.

Esha pushed up from the chair and walked to the tub. It had already been filled with water. That was the job of the youngest in the camp, those training in the hopes of holding the mantle of Ranger someday. Esha remembered those days. They had been long and grueling, but they had molded her into the warrior she was today.

She waved her hand over the water, calling to her magic. Yellow smoke with a trace of gold burst from her palm and wrapped around the copper tub as her magic heated the liquid. When the temperature satisfied her, she ended her magic and undressed to climb into the water.

Esha leaned back against the tub with a sigh. As she soaked, tendrils of heat curled up from the surface. She watched them as she thought about the day. She *had* overstepped when it came to telling Kendrick they would work with him. It had been wrong of her to do that, especially in front of her Rangers. Had she done it because Savita was her sister? Esha would never have thought herself capable of disregarding a Reader, even her sibling.

Yet she had.

Kendrick had shifted in front of them. They had all seen it. Shapeshifters existed. They knew nothing about them because elves had always thought they were a myth. Add to that the fact that Kendrick was also a dragon, and Esha's mind had spun with excitement. It was the first time in her life she had forgotten her training and position. She had simply reacted.

That might be fine during battle, but it couldn't happen again. Not in front of her squad. And definitely not with her sister.

She didn't doubt that Savita would punish her more than sending Kendrick away in three days. The *how* would be left up to her sister's discretion. Savita had the power to remove Esha as a Ranger. Permanently.

That thought left Esha cold. Being a Ranger was everything she had ever wanted. Could *ever* want. Esha shivered, even in the heat of the water. Whatever had overtaken her earlier couldn't happen a second time. She wanted Kendrick and the Dragon Kings as allies. She also sought to catch the thing that killed so indiscriminately. There had to be a way for her to have both without being stripped of her title as Ranger. Surely, her sister wouldn't do that to her. Would she?

Esha knew how vengeful Savita could be, though. She had seen it. No one else in the camp had. They believed Savita the serene, unruffled Reader she portrayed. Savita had a long memory, she never forgot anyone who wronged her, and she rarely forgave anything.

In many ways, Savita was like the Dark Elves in that regard. Esha had made the mistake of telling her sister that one time. It was the first—and last—time Esha had ever done that. Savita had struck viciously, using magic and her fists to pummel Esha. They had been young, but Esha had never forgotten it.

Savita was far from finished with her. Esha would have to watch every step she made and consider every word she said. Many in her squad joked that it must be nice that she and Savita watched each other's backs, but that was far from the truth.

Savita cared about her position above all else. And she couldn't have anyone thinking someone had challenged her. Yet Esha had forgotten that and spoke out of turn.

Because of Kendrick.

It all came back to him. Even now, knowing her position could be in jeopardy, she couldn't stop thinking about him. If she were smart, she'd send another squad to work with him tomorrow.

But she wasn't that smart.

Esha planned to be a part of history—even if Savita stripped her of her rank and position.

Chapter Nine

Kendrick stared out over the calm water. He couldn't put it off any longer. He had to notify Constantine. He had hoped Esha would return so he could pose more questions, but she didn't show. He was more upset by that than expected.

The world of the elves was fascinating, and he knew he had just scratched the surface of all there was to know. His inquisitiveness bordered on obsessive. Though Esha had made it sound as if elven magic weren't as great as dragon, he had a feeling it was more than most on Zora. And if there were elves, what else resided on the planet that no one knew about?

Kendrick opened his mental link. *"Con,"* he called.

The King of Dragon Kings responded quickly. *"I was just about to contact you."*

"Is everything all right?"

"We've had a visitor to Cairnkeep."

The capital of the dragon land, a stunning place in the mountains, was where Eurwen and Brandr ruled. Something in Con's voice gave Kendrick pause. *"Anything urgent?"*

"You could say that. Ceri told us about this morning."

"Who is Ceri?"

"You mean you doona know the name of the Pink you've been talking to these past weeks?"

"So, that's her name." Kendrick chuckled. Then he sobered. *"Did you say she came to you?"*

"Aye. After she saw you tangle with the threat we've been tracking."

Kendrick briefly closed his eyes, remorse and shame choking him. He'd forgotten the Pink had been there watching all of it.

"We were all getting ready to head your way. All of us. Because we feared you were injured—or worse."

Kendrick felt like a jerk for waiting to check in. "Fuck, Con. I'm sorry. I'm fine. But I did tangle with that thing."

"We knew that much," Con snapped.

Kendrick ran a hand down his face and thought back to the day's events. "I apologize. My intent was to gather as much intel as I could before telling you about them."

"About who? My patience is running out. First Merrill, and now you do this?"

Kendrick grimaced. He took Con's anger because he deserved it. But he would make it up to everyone. "The being I fought did to me what it did to the others. It struck me with magic. I didna have any physical injuries, but I sure felt its punch. It jerked me out of dragon form, and I couldna shift for some time after. I thought I was getting the advantage by using my other senses, but it soon got me entangled. In my haste to take it down, I let my emotions cloud my judgment. I thought about the dragons that had been killed and the Kings who had been injured, and I thought of Merrill."

"We doona know if it's responsible for Merrill or no'," Con said in a neutral voice.

"I know." Kendrick paused for a heartbeat. "I acted recklessly, and I know better. But that decision gained us something."

Con sighed. "We're all feeling the pressure of this. It's making me question whether we should patrol alone."

"I admit, my actions were questionable, but the end result isna."

"Are you telling me you discovered how to beat it?"

"I wish. Nay, when I crossed the border, I discovered the people on the other side—or should I say the elves on the other side. That's the them I mentioned earlier."

"Elves?" Con asked, surprise coloring his words.

Kendrick chuckled. "I was just as shocked. They joined the skirmish when that thing had me pinned down. I'm no' sure I would've gotten away had they no' come upon me. I talked them into allowing me to stay so we could work together to hunt this thing. They've been after it for a while."

"Do they know who you are?"

"They do. They hadna seen a dragon in some time—thought they were gone. No one ventures close to the border, and they thought shifters were a myth."

Con made a sound in the back of his throat. "Just as we thought of elves."

"Aye. It's a tenuous venture for the moment. Their culture is verra complex. The group I'm with calls themselves the Asavori Rangers. They're warriors and made up of different classes of elves."

"Are they potential allies?"

"I think so. It's going to take some trust building on both sides, however. This place is stunning. I want to stay and cultivate a relationship. The leader of this group of Rangers, Esha, seems open to the idea. Though her sister, Savita, a rune Reader, makes the decisions."

Con grunted. *"I gather she's no' keen on an alliance."*

"No' really."

"Can you win her over?"

"I'm going to try."

"What of their magic? Is it powerful?"

Kendrick wrinkled his nose as he thought about it. *"I've no' seen it. Esha was surprised at mine. She said elves couldna match it."*

"Doona take her word for it."

"I doona intend to. Now, do you want to know about Shecrish and the elves?"

"Absolutely."

For the next hour, Kendrick relayed the information he had gained and answered resulting questions. As expected, Con was interested in the elves. An alliance between their two cultures could help if there were a war. How far that pact could go was up to Eurwen and Brandr.

Sooner or later, the elves would likely ask to cross the boundary and travel across the land of the dragons, just as he was doing here. And Kendrick knew that would never be allowed. There was a reason the dragons remained separate from everyone else on the realm. Kendrick would have to share that story with Esha in hopes she appreciated the rationale.

"Keep in regular contact," Con told him as their conversation wrapped up.

"I will. Also, tell Ceri I appreciate her concern."

Con chuckled. *"She's no' exactly thrilled to learn she's been worried for nothing."*

"I've been trying to get her to talk to me since I arrived. She wouldna even tell me her name."

"Seems you made more of an impact than you thought."

Kendrick grinned as he thought about the tiny dragon. *"I'll make it up to her."*

"That would probably be wise. I doona need to tell you to be safe, do I?"

"You know me."

"Exactly."

Kendrick wore a smile when Con severed the link between them. So, the Pink had been concerned. And now he knew her name. He was under no illusions that Ceri would talk to him when he returned, especially after this. He wouldn't give up, though.

His gaze traveled slowly around him. Esha hadn't come back. He also hadn't had another visit from the Dark Elf, Dain. But Kendrick wasn't alone. He sensed others out there. Most likely Rangers who had been sent to keep an eye on him. He had given his word that he would stay in his camp until Esha came for him. The Rangers had no reason to trust him, but he would show them they could.

His thoughts turned to Savita. That's where his concerns lay. She could sway Esha's enthusiasm for hunting their shared foe with him. The three days she had given him weren't long enough, but he had to plan on it being all he would get. Sure, he could tell them all to kiss off and remain for as long as he liked, but he wouldn't. Not only because he was trying to build trust but also because war was already brewing on the dragons' eastern border. He didn't want a separate conflict to the west.

Kendrick ignored the comfortable bed within the yurt and stretched out on the ground. He threaded his fingers behind his head and looked at the midnight sky and the stars blinking down at him while the rainforest animals filled the night with their own special music. New constellations stared back at him. He wanted to learn what they were. Surely, someone on the realm would know. Maybe even an elf. He filed that away to talk to Esha about in the morning.

* * * *

Dawn broke with Savita's stomach still tied in knots. She had consulted the runes multiple times throughout the night, and the answer was always the same. *Danger.*

No matter the question she posed, no matter the context.

Her conversations with Esha and the Dragon King had gone as poorly as she'd known they would. But it wasn't as if she'd had a choice. Her sister clearly didn't realize the consequences of her actions. All Esha saw was a way to achieve her goal of finding the thing that'd killed their people. Yet there was so much more to it. Not that Savita could tell her any of that.

Then there was Kendrick. A shapeshifter. A Dragon King. Her superiors would want to know about him immediately. Savita hadn't yet shared that information, though she wouldn't be able to hold off much longer.

She walked to the mirror that hung in her tent and stared at her reflection, taking in the paint on her face and the gold designs that marked her as a Reader. She had rubbed her cheeks so much during the long night that the paint had smeared. Instead of calling in her maid, Savita stripped, pinned up her hair, and washed herself in the large tub without heating the water. The chilly bath was bracing and helped to invigorate her.

After she dressed, she brushed out her hair until it gleamed. Then she sat before the mirror to apply the paint and markings again. She couldn't remember the last time she had gone without them. As she stared at her now-bare face, she almost didn't recognize herself. Her identity was that of a Reader.

The life of a little girl who had been thrilled to have a younger sister felt like a lifetime ago. So much had transpired since then. She had left the family and immersed herself in all that came with being a Reader. It was her life and all she'd ever wanted. The power of her position was simply a byproduct of her ability to understand the runes.

A Reader never allowed themselves to become emotionally involved with an outcome given by the runes. Savita had held to that standard and never found it difficult to keep herself distant.

Except for one time.

Savita closed her eyes as she turned her thoughts away from that event. It was a secret she carried within her. There was always a chance the runes would tell another Reader, but that hadn't happened so far.

And yet, Savita found herself in a similar position now.

She sighed, opened her eyes, and looked into the copper orbs staring back at her, noting the flecks of gold shimmering in her irises. She picked up the pot of gold paint and began applying it to her face with her special brush in slow, sure strokes.

With every sweep, she became the renowned Reader that many had sought. She had a duty, and nothing could make her forget that. Not even the arrival of a Dragon King.

Chapter Ten

There was a pep in Esha's step when she emerged from her tent. Her excitement died a little when she looked for her squad and couldn't find them.

"Sister."

At the sound of Savita's voice behind her, Esha turned. "Where is my team?"

"Elsewhere."

"You do understand that I'm in charge of my crew, right? We each have a place. You don't want me interfering with yours, and I don't want you interfering with mine."

Savita stood calmly as she said, "The runes made the decision, not me."

"Did they? Or is this you showing me how you can put me in my place?"

A brief frown marred Savita's brow. "I read the runes. That's all."

Esha took a step closer and lowered her voice as anger made it shake. "That's far from what you do. You're supposed to be here to *help*."

"I am."

"By sending my team away when you've given me only three days to hunt the creature with Kendrick? Forgive me if I don't believe you."

Savita swallowed and glanced to the side. "Follow me."

Esha remained after her sister had pivoted and walked away. She wanted to ignore her like she used to do when they were younger, but she couldn't. Esha might lead the Rangers, but Savita could exercise command when the runes spoke to her. Was her sister lying? Others accused Readers of it, but no one had ever been able to prove it happened. Esha knew she had little chance of that herself. Yet it seemed suspicious that Savita had made such a move after their clash yesterday.

With her jaw clenched, Esha followed Savita into her tent. She found her sister standing before the table she used to read the runes. On it were

Savita's white runes, their gold markings clear. There were twenty-eight of them, each marked with a specific symbol.

Esha crossed her arms over her chest. "Why are you showing me these? You know I can't read them."

"I get the same response for every question I pose."

"Which is?" Esha pushed when Savita fell silent.

Her sister's copper gaze was unwavering. "Danger."

"And you think that's Kendrick, I suppose?"

"I don't know who or what it is. I've asked about Kendrick. I get that response. I asked about working with him, I get that response. I asked about the thing you're hunting, I get that response. I ask if anyone is going to attack us, I get that response. I ask if it's going to rain, I get that response. I ask if we'll catch lots of fish for dinner tonight..."

"You get that response. I get it," Esha said as her arms fell to her sides. "Is that normal?"

Savita braced her hands on the table and looked at the runes. "Never. The answers might be similar, but never so exact."

"Ask those questions again."

"I did," Savita replied as she looked up. "Dozens of times throughout the night."

Esha gazed at the runes for a heartbeat. "The runes agreed with my assessment to hunt the foe."

"They did."

"They've not changed their mind, have they?"

Savita's lips twisted. "It isn't that simple."

"It is. Of course, there's danger each time I take my squad out of camp. Danger is what being a Ranger is about. If the runes aren't telling you that we should stop hunting, then we don't."

"The danger it's warning me about should be taken into consideration."

Esha rolled her eyes. "It's telling you that for everything."

"I'm aware," Savita said tightly.

Esha licked her lips and lowered her voice. "Are you sure you can still read them?"

Anger sparked in her sister's eyes. Savita pointed to the table and spoke in a clipped tone. "Look at the runes. Look at each of them. Memorize their placements."

Esha did as her sister asked.

Then Savita gathered the stones and put them into their bag. Savita shook the bag as she held Esha's gaze. Her sister asked in a clear voice,

"Should Esha continue hunting the entity that's killing elves?" Then she opened the bag and dumped the runes.

Esha's mouth dropped open as she watched each stone come to rest in exactly the same position as before.

"Now do you understand?" Savita demanded.

Esha nodded. "I do."

"And you're still going to Kendrick?"

"I am. The runes tell you of danger, but not what kind, where it's coming from, or even when. I can't sit here, doing nothing as I wait. No Ranger would."

Savita's expression fell. "I know."

"If something changes, let me know."

"Will you return tonight?"

Esha considered that before she shook her head. "You gave us three days. We need to cover a lot of ground. And, unfortunately, we don't even know where to begin. There isn't time for me to come back to camp."

"I'm asking you not to go with Kendrick."

Esha heard the carefully worded request. Savita was worried, and while she might agree with Savita, Esha wouldn't remain. She couldn't. "Elves are dying. I'm going to do something about that."

"I know." Savita sighed, her shoulders drooping. "Be safe."

"I'll see you in a few days."

Esha walked out of the tent and the camp. Her sister's distress over the runes was troubling, but it could mean literally anything. Esha lengthened her strides as she walked through the dense forest. She glanced at the positions of Rangers who stood on guard. The Wood Elves were high in the trees, while other elves had hidden themselves elsewhere. She felt their gazes on her as she picked her way to Kendrick. The closer she got, the more her mood lightened. From the moment she had opened her eyes that morning, she had been excited to see him and learn more about dragons—and him.

As she approached the lake, she saw his fire through the trees. She emerged from the jungle. Her gaze swept the area without seeing him. She then looked at the round structure and couldn't help but wonder if he was sleeping. Was he on his back, his stomach, or his side? Would his hair be mussed? What would he look like after just opening his eyes?

Did he sleep naked?

The thought made her heart skip a beat. Esha took a step in the direction of the tent when she heard a sound from the lake. Her head swung toward the water as Kendrick's head broke the surface. Water sluiced over his face. He shook his head, causing droplets to fly from the ends of his hair. A wide grin spread over his face when he noticed her.

"Good morning," he called as he treaded water.

She walked to the shoreline, doing her best not to notice the way his muscular shoulders lifted from the lake. But it was impossible. "There could've been something dangerous in the water."

"Could have," he replied as he swam toward her. His arms were strong and sure as he moved effortlessly to the shore.

She swallowed hard. No one had ever made swimming look so sexy. Every little peek she got of him made her want to see all of him—every gorgeous inch. Esha was acutely aware of how fast her breathing had become. Even as she told herself to look away, she silently begged to see more.

Then he stopped swimming and wiped the water from his face with his hands. It took her a minute to realize that he was walking through the water.

"I'd like to think you would've told me. There are some creatures I've never seen before. The lavender animal with the long snout. What is that?"

Esha chuckled and forced her eyes to his face and not the corded muscles of his neck and shoulders. "A lundu. It's a curious animal who often swims with others."

"Aye. That would explain why it stayed beside me after I entered the loch."

Unable to look away, her eyes dropped to the water as it met him. Blood began to rush loudly in her ears when more of his expansive chest appeared. It held her transfixed. She was utterly mesmerized by the sight of Kendrick. Her lips parted as she struggled to draw breath into her lungs, even as the water lowered to the rippling muscles of his stomach. She could count each one. Then even lower to his trim waist and hips to a line of dark hair that led to... She jerked her head to the side the instant she realized he was naked.

Esha sucked in mouthfuls of air, hating herself for looking away even as an image of him filled her mind. He was everything she had imagined he would be.

"Apologies," Kendrick said. "I'm dressed now."

Esha hated that she had missed a perfect opportunity to see his glorious body. She wasn't sure why she had looked away to begin with. It wasn't as if she hadn't seen males naked before. She drew in a steadying breath and slowly looked at him. His clothes might cover that incredible body, but she couldn't erase the image of his skin glistening with water in the morning sun. Or the way his green eyes had burned.

It took Esha three tries to find her voice. When she did, it still sounded breathless and…needy. "It's fine." But it wasn't. Not when wanton desire scorched through her so urgently.

"Are Rangers celibate?"

Conversation. That was exactly what she needed to help turn her mind away from such lustful thoughts. She forced a smile until his words penetrated. This wasn't what she wanted to discuss. Esha cleared her throat. "We have sex as often as we want. The caveat being that we never have the same partner more than once. Not as long as we're Rangers. We serve as Rangers first and foremost. There can never be any entanglements."

"What happens if you fall in love?"

"It's rare that it happens, but if and when it does, the elf leaves the Rangers."

Kendrick raked a hand through his still-wet hair. "That's a wee bit harsh."

"That rule is there for a reason. We spend years out here. We can't be thinking about a family or anything that could divide our attention."

"What if two Rangers fall in love?"

She shrugged. "It has happened. Both were relieved of duty. We take steps so the chances of that are minimal. While we're not forbidden from taking a fellow Ranger as a lover, it can't be someone on our same team. Being a Ranger is serious business. Too many count on us. We have to be utterly devoted to our mission."

"I can understand and appreciate that."

But she felt the need to elaborate. "Most join the Rangers because they've devoted their lives to it. There are those who stay for a short while and then leave, those who stay for a long while before they depart, and those who remain until they die."

His green eyes held hers. "Which are you?"

"The Rangers are my life. I will be one until I die."

Kendrick smiled as he nodded, accepting her words. "Where would you like to start today?"

She was grateful for the change of subject. She didn't understand why she was suddenly angry. He had done nothing to warrant it, and she wasn't even sure if she *was* irritated at him. Maybe it was more directed at herself. After all, he had been all she could think about since they'd met. Then seeing him this morning…well, that was something she'd thought she could handle. Turned out she couldn't.

Esha wanted him. She shut her mind to those thoughts and looked away from his prying eyes. "We could return to where we found you yesterday."

"I didna see anything there that might lead us in a direction. Did you?"

Esha shook her head. "I could take you to the last place it struck here."

"Let's start by you telling me all the places it has attacked and when."

"To see how far apart the assaults were?"

He grinned. "Exactly. I'd also like to see if any of the areas or those hit have anything in common. Did everyone die?"

"Sadly, yes. No one could tell us how they were struck or exactly when."

"Do you have a map?"

Esha's lips curved in excitement. "I do."

She rubbed her hands together, warming them as her magic shifted through her. Then she drew her palms apart as they faced each other. Golden ribbons of magic wove around her hands and arms as a three-dimensional map of the plateau began to weave itself together. The wider she spread her hands, the larger the map grew.

Kendrick moved closer, his gaze intent on the image. "The plateau is larger than I thought."

"It's significant in size," she agreed. Her gaze moved around the edges, following Kendrick's as he noted the shape of it.

The transparent, gold-hued map hovered in the air between them. Esha pointed to the first place the entity had attacked. As she touched the illustration, a dark mark appeared there to indicate the position. She proceeded to do that with four other locations.

Kendrick crossed his arms over his chest, his brow furrowed as he studied the map intently. "Where are we?"

She marked it. "And we found you here," she said, adding another mark near the border.

"It has struck near cities, water, forests, and out in the open. I can see nothing that determines a pattern."

She nodded in agreement. "We also got word last week that a group of Mountain Elves battled something in their region. They lost four of their people."

"It doesn't seem to have a preference for where it attacks. Is it merely opportunity motivated?"

"If that were the case, why hasn't it struck us?"

Kendrick raised his gaze to meet hers. "Good point. Could it be looking for something?"

"I suppose. What about with the attacks on dragons? What did it do?"

His lips flattened in a line for a moment. "Until you told me about the deaths here, we were sure it was after us specifically. It killed several dragons at once no' so long ago, and in a way, that seemed entirely too easy. Then it went after Eurwen."

The sound of the woman's name made Esha's heart skip a beat. She had never asked if Kendrick had someone in his life. Just because he was here alone didn't mean his heart didn't belong to someone. Her throat felt thick as she asked, "Is that your wife?"

"She's one of the twins who rules the dragons. Eurwen is a Dragon Queen, while Brandr is a King."

Esha's eyebrows rose with interest. "There are Queens, then?"

Kendrick grinned. "Aye, lass." But that smile vanished in the next breath. "It took hold of Eurwen, keeping her locked inside her mind. At least that's how she described it. She couldna move until she broke free of that. I wondered how that was possible, but I felt it yesterday. The difference was, it seemed to want more from Eurwen. When the entity came after Brandr, her twin, it was a swift attack. Same with Cullen and Shaw, my fellow Kings. It knocked them from the sky as it did me. All of us were in dragon form at the time, and the magic it hit us with caused us to return to this form."

"That doesn't sound feasible."

"I wish it wasna. When Cullen fought it, he said a wildcat appeared and seemed to be able to see the being. Once the cat attacked, the thing vanished. You doona happen to have any wildcats here, do you?"

Esha shook her head. "No, but I do like that you found something that was able to see it. Maybe other animals can."

"Potentially. I'd really like to know why we can no'."

"Agreed. It's hard to battle something you can't see coming at you. You said you felt its magic, but you didn't have any injuries."

Distaste colored his expression. "I hope you never feel it. Because while it might no' leave a mark, the damage is extensive."

"No elf is left who could describe it. I'd like to know everything. Tell me more, please."

"What I feel may no' be what you feel."

She shrugged and grinned. "It's better to know something."

Chapter Eleven

Kendrick ran his hand over his lower jaw. Elves might look similar to humans, but that was probably where the parallels ended. If the being that attacked him could dole out such devastating hits to him, then Esha needed to be prepared.

"As you said, there were no visible wounds," he began. "It doesna pierce as, say, your sword would. Instead, it seeps through the skin and attacks the muscles, bones, and organs. It felt as if someone had taken my muscles and wrenched them apart, then went after my bones, pulverizing them."

Her brow furrowed as she listened. "When we came upon you, you were on the ground."

"Aye. That thing was wrapped around me—or its magic was. I couldna tell which. All I know is that I couldna move. It had me pinned."

Her shoulders lifted as she took a deep breath. "I've not seen you in battle, but I have witnessed your abilities," she said as she jerked her chin to the yurt. "The fact that it hindered you so is worrying."

"A dragon's magic is verra powerful, some of the most formidable there is, but there is always something that has more." Kendrick and the others had never experienced that before on Earth, but as he had to keep reminding himself…Zora wasn't Earth. It was something altogether different.

As was the stunning woman before him.

"You appeared to heal quickly enough."

Kendrick thought about how he hadn't been able to shift after the attack. That had terrified him more than anything because nothing had ever prevented him from going to his true form before. It was something their enemies would love to know, which was why he didn't tell Esha about it. He didn't want it getting out to anyone.

"Though there were no outward injuries," she continued, unaware of his thoughts, "you moved as though you were unharmed. Was that an act?"

He grinned and shrugged. "Partly. I had no idea who you and your team were. You did come to my aid, but for all I knew, you were also an enemy."

"Right."

"The magic it used didna leave me quickly. It remained for some time. Even though my body heals almost instantly from any wounds, this magic was different."

Her brows drew together. "We don't heal that way. Which means we try not to let it use its magic on us."

"If we can find a way to see it, then you can devise a way to kill it."

"That's a big *if*. We don't know where it lives, why it attacks, or even what it is." She looked down at the map before her. "I'm a good tracker, but this thing doesn't leave any trail to follow."

Kendrick lowered his gaze to the map. He looked between the areas where the attacks had occurred, following each in succession in the order of when they happened. "Are there any classes of elves it hasn't killed?"

"Sea Elves. And Dark Elves. At least that we know of."

He shook his head as he continued searching for something on the map that would give them a clue. "When it first attacked us, we didn't hear of any humans being harmed. That was why we thought it was just after us."

"Is it only seeking out those with magic?"

Kendrick met her gaze. "It could be, but there were humans with magic that were no' touched either."

"Could it be human, then?"

"At this point, it could be anything."

Her lips twisted ruefully. "Three days isn't going to be enough time."

"Nay, it isna." He paused for a moment and then asked, "Why did Savita put such a time limit?"

Esha threw up her hands and rolled her eyes. "I don't know."

"Was she verra cross last night?"

"You could say that."

"Could that be the reason?"

Esha released a long sigh. "I asked her the same question. She told me it was the runes."

"I doona mean to be disparaging, but could she be lying?"

"Don't worry. I thought that, too. There's no way to tell. I know she's upset. Before I left this morn, she told me that everything she asked the runes resulted in the same answer."

"Which was?" he pressed.

"Danger."

Kendrick frowned at that news. "Everything?"

"Everything. To prove it, she made me memorize the runes and where they lay on the table. Then she asked a question, and they landed in exactly the same positions."

"That doesna seem as if that would happen."

"It doesn't. It's why she's so upset," Esha said.

Kendrick motioned to the map. "I can see no rhyme or reason to the attacks, but there is considerable danger in us going after this foe. I heard my friends describe the experience, and I didna heed their words when I went after it."

"Are you trying to talk me out of hunting it?"

He heard the warning in her words as he searched her golden-amber gaze. "I only want to be clear on what could happen. I doona know your physical abilities or hindrances. I doona know what will happen when we encounter the entity."

"I know not to use my eyes," she said with a grin.

Kendrick couldn't help but chuckle. "It wouldna do any good. No' really. I saw what looked like a ripple across water out of the corner of my eye, but this thing moves quickly and silently."

"Makes me wish we had a wildcat."

"They're no' exactly pets."

She shrugged as if that didn't matter. "We need an advantage, which we don't have."

"No' now. What we do have is choices for where to begin. What are your thoughts?"

Esha bit her bottom lip as she looked at the map again. After a silent moment, she said, "Your guess is as good as mine."

"Then let's head out. We might get lucky." Either way, he would see more of their country, and perhaps even one of the cities. "Do we need to wait on the rest of your team?"

She couldn't quite meet his gaze. "It's just the two of us."

He was taken aback by her words. Kendrick would've thought that Savita wouldn't want the two of them alone. Or had Esha initiated it? Regardless, he was happy about it. Nothing like spending some time alone with a beautiful elf. Especially one who looked at him with such heat in her eyes. His balls tightened just thinking about it.

Kendrick cleared his throat and quickly shifted his thoughts to the current conversation. "What happened?"

"My sister," was all Esha said. She turned her head to his lodgings. "What about that?"

With a thought, Kendrick made the yurt and the fire vanish.

"Do you use such magic all the time?"

He shook his head. "Actually, we make a point of doing a lot without magic, but there are times when it comes in handy."

"I bet."

"You don't use such magic?"

"Not like you. We use our hands to erect buildings."

"Then how do you use magic?"

She paused. "For me, the sun enhances my magic. It helps in battle."

"Battle magic?"

"Something like that. We don't use magic to create things but rather to enrich them."

Kendrick nodded. "I can no' wait to see more."

Their gazes held for another moment.

Esha was the first to look away. She motioned to the map. "Let's head east toward the river."

"Can we make our way there this way?" he asked as he drew a diagonal from their location to the bisected area where the river lay. It would bring him closer to Rannora and grant him a better look at the city.

Esha raised her hands on either side of the map, then pushed her palms together, shrinking the image until it was gone. "We can, but it will take some time. The forests are thick. There's no easy way to go through them. Do you think the entity is there, or do you just want to see Rannora?"

"I'd like to see the city, aye."

She nodded tightly.

"If you're worried that I'll shift in front of your people, I willna."

"That might be wise. You saw how my squad reacted."

He had. "I doona want to cause any panic."

She glanced at him before heading around the lake. Kendrick fell into step beside her. He looked at the sky. He wished he could fly. That would not only give him a better view of the plateau but would also allow them to get wherever they wanted to go faster. Everything he saw now made him think of Earth before the humans arrived and cut down forests to build and cover the ground with roadways and concrete. He drew in a deep breath and let the splendor fill every pore.

Esha's gaze was focused ahead as they walked. "Do you have the same magic in both forms? What I mean is, do you have more magic when you're in your true form?"

"The magic is pretty much the same."

"But you can do other things in your true form?"

He inwardly grinned. "All dragons breathe fire. It isna something we do in this form, though I've never tried. What about your people? Does everyone have the same magic?"

"Not exactly. Each class has a specialty, of sorts. For instance, as I mentioned, Wood Elves are good with animals."

"What are Sun Elves good at?"

She shot him a look, a smile playing about her lips. "Bringing light when it's needed."

"That could come in handy." He liked this question-and-answer exchange. "Do you get ill?"

"Sometimes. Do dragons?"

"Sometimes."

"Not Kings, though."

He laughed. "Nay, no' Kings. What about healing from injuries?"

"We die easier than you, if that's what you're wondering. Star Elves are excellent healers if it is not something grave, but we're hearty. Star Elves are always needed, so they got used to moving around. I suppose they grew to love being nomadic. It's also why you'll always find at least one Star Elf in every Ranger squad. Do you have anything like that?"

Kendrick shook his head. "You could say we have classes, too. We call them clans."

"I like that."

They shared a smile before each turned their attention back to the path before them. The heat was oppressive, and sweat soon covered Kendrick. He used his sleeve to wipe his face. Esha didn't seem bothered at all. Then the rain began, a steady stream that soon had them both drenched. The canopy helped to shield them somewhat, but it was so hot that Kendrick enjoyed the rain.

"The clans were separated by color," he continued as he stared up at a group of animals that jumped from one tree to another. They moved fast, hidden amongst branches heavy with leaves for camouflage.

"Did the dragons always stay in their groups?"

"More often than no', aye. There wasna a decree, though. More like everyone just knew to stay in their clan. At least, they used to. Do yours mix?"

Her nose wrinkled. "Not often. You see it more in the cities, but it's different in rural areas. Can dragons have babies?"

"Aye."

A small frown puckered her brow for a heartbeat. "Do you know if the dragons were brought here as we were?"

"They were no'." He felt her gaze on him as they walked. He didn't mind telling her the tale, but he worried how she and other elves might take it.

"You know why we were brought here, don't you?"

Kendrick halted and met her gaze as she stopped. "We're trying to determine why infants are brought to this realm. If I knew, I promise I'd tell you."

"Humans, elves, and dragons," Esha said in a soft voice as her gaze slid away. "Do you know if there are any other beings out there?"

"There are Banshees and an Amazon. I also suspect there are even more."

"What is a Banshee and Amazon?"

"Banshees know when someone is about to die. For Tamlyn, she knows when a child of magic is about to die."

"That sounds horrible," she said, her face wrinkled in distaste.

Kendrick nodded. "It is. The Amazon are women warriors. They're taller than most females and are experts with weapons."

Esha grinned. "I'd like to meet one."

"Maybe you'll be able to."

Without a word, Esha started walking again. The terrain became more difficult, and the conversation ended. He didn't push her to answer more questions. They had three days. For now, he filed away each animal he spotted and the sheer size of the rainforest. After about an hour, the rain stopped.

They passed many lakes, some big, others small. There were splashes in the water, and he wanted to know what kind of aquatic life was beneath the surface, but that would have to wait. The lush plateau offered a plethora of plants and animals. Esha paused beside a tree and picked a piece of fruit. She tossed him one before taking one for herself.

He watched as she bit into it and kept walking. Kendrick followed her example and was amazed at the slightly sweet and juicy fruit. There were many more fruits they passed. Esha pointed out the ones he could try, and he took every opportunity. They ranged from sweet to sour to bitter.

They paused beside a lake for a drink. After Esha had her fill, she asked, "Who is looking after your clan while you're here?"

Kendrick tried not to feel the pang in his heart at the reminder that he no longer had dragons to rule, but it was impossible. He flicked the water from his hand and sat back on his haunches as he looked at the lake.

"You don't have to tell me." She stood.

"It isna an easy question to answer." Kendrick slid his gaze to her and climbed to his feet to follow her as she started walking again. "It's…complicated."

Esha jumped over a fallen tree and waited for him to join her. "Are you no longer a King?"

"I'm still a Dragon King, but the dragons here are no longer in clans. They live where they want, with whoever they want."

"*Here*," she repeated. "You've said that before. Almost like there's another place you're comparing it to."

Kendrick nodded as they continued walking. "I'm no' from Zora."

Esha didn't show any outward signs that she was surprised by his words. "How did you get here?"

"Through a Fae doorway that links my world to this one."

"A doorway? I don't understand."

He shrugged. "It's Fae magic, which I can no' explain. Some are powerful enough to teleport from place to place, but most use doorways they craft with their magic. It's like a wormhole that connects two places."

"And they can do that between worlds?"

"Some can, aye."

"That's unbelievable. So, why are you on Zora?"

"Because of the dragons."

"You want to bring them to your realm?"

He drew in a breath. "It's a long story."

"We have a long walk."

Kendrick ran a hand through his damp hair. "I did promise to tell you about the dragons."

"I want to know all there is," she said. "But you don't look like you wish to talk about it."

"It isna a good story." But he would tell her as he'd promised. "The dragons on Zora are descendants from my realm, Earth. There, we once inhabited every corner of the planet. And we thrived." He thought back to his time as a youngling and finding his way in the clan. "Things were no' what I would call easy, but they were good. That was how it had been for eons before I was born and for a time after I became a King."

"Then what happened?"

He twisted his lips ruefully. "Humans arrived on our planet. All adults. And all terrified. Constantine, the King of Dragon Kings, gathered all the Kings together, and we went to the mortals."

"I don't imagine that went well."

Kendrick chuckled despite himself. "It didna. They were terrified. Can you imagine a bunch of dragons standing before you?"

"I know my reaction at just seeing one."

He was glad that she helped to lighten this retelling. Otherwise, he knew he could get mired in his resentment. "That was the first time any of us shifted to this form. The magic of Earth gave us the ability so we could communicate with the mortals. We offered them shelter, vowing to keep them safe. That pledge was our undoing."

Chapter Twelve

His words left Esha cold. She almost told him he didn't have to finish, but she wanted to know. "How?"

"We were foolish enough to believe we could all live in harmony."

She winced at the anger that deepened his voice. She didn't need to prod him to continue. He did that on his own.

"At first, things were good. We carved out land for the humans—there was only a handful of them. But they bred so quickly. It seemed as if they were asking for more and more land all the time. Each of the Kings gave up parcels of their domain for the mortals, but it was never enough."

She noticed that Kendrick's breathing had quickened. He had his hands fisted at his sides, and a muscle pulsed in his jaw.

"The humans said a dragon started the conflict by eating one of them. Dragons claimed the mortals hunted the smaller ones. No one knows when it began, only that it erupted into dispute after dispute. We know dragons fed on humans. We know humans hunted and killed dragons. Which of those was in retaliation, we could never figure out. We Kings worked out a treaty with them, and peace returned for a short while. Meanwhile, most Kings were helping mortals build cities. Many, I included, took humans as lovers. One of us, Ulrik, wanted to have one as his mate."

"You make that sound as if it was wrong."

Kendrick glanced at her, lifting a shoulder in a shrug. "A dragon knows its mate. We mate for life, however long that is. In the years since the humans arrived, no' one gave birth to a live bairn. Most miscarried within days or weeks of becoming pregnant. The few who did carry to term had stillborn babes."

Esha didn't know what it was like to give birth, but she could well imagine the agony of a child being born dead.

"That knowledge meant that if Ulrik took her as his mate, he would never have children," Kendrick said. "We still supported him. Unbeknownst to us, however, Ulrik's jealous uncle had set a plan into motion that tricked the human Ulrik had fallen for, getting her to agree to kill Ulrik. Con learned of the plan and told the rest of us."

Esha cringed as she glanced at Kendrick. "What happened?"

"Ulrik was like a brother to Con and one of the best of us. He was kind and generous. Of anyone to be betrayed, it never should have been him. Compound that with the decades of issues we'd experienced with the mortals, and we knew something had to be done. We tracked down the human who was set to betray him, and we...we killed her."

Esha cut her gaze to him and watched Kendrick carefully, imagining herself in his place if she were told someone would betray Savita in such a way. She knew she would track them down herself—and she would stop them.

Kendrick met her gaze.

"Everyone reaches a breaking point. Even Dragon Kings," she said.

He nodded slowly and slid his gaze away. "Once Ulrik found out, he became enraged. He was furious at us, but we were no' the ones he took it out on. You're right. We each have a breaking point, and that night, we all snapped in different ways. We had blood on our hands. Human blood. But Ulrik's pain went much deeper."

"Because he loved her."

"Aye," Kendrick whispered. "We thought we had saved one of our own, and in a way, we had. But we'd also started a war that we had been fighting to prevent for many years. When Ulrik took his Silvers and attacked the humans, many joined him. We wanted our realm back. The smaller dragon clans had been decimated to critical levels. We were tired of our lands shrinking and the mortals demanding more. We were just...tired of it all."

He walked for a bit in silence. Esha had slowed her strides as she listened. There was so much sadness and ire within Kendrick that it made her heart hurt.

"So many died," he said. "I still hear their screams, still smell their blood. I think I always will."

Esha didn't know what to say. Kendrick appeared lost in his memories, and she regretted asking him to delve into them now.

After another quiet period, he shook himself. "Con was the only one who didna go after the mortals. Eventually, he brought each of us back to his side. That was when we saw what we had done. The magic chose each of us because we were the strongest of our clans, the ones with the purest of hearts. And we had done…that. Con reminded us of the vow we'd taken when the humans arrived. So, we ordered our dragons to protect the villages and cities. We were saving the mortals, but they didna care. They…attacked the dragons. And the dragons who were told no' to harm them did nothing as humans slaughtered them. *Those* are the screams and cries I hear the loudest."

A tear fell onto Esha's cheek. She felt Kendrick's pain as if it were hers. She might not have been there, might not have witnessed the horror, but she felt it.

"We knew whatever peace we'd had would never return," he told her. "To the mortals, we were monsters who had to be killed, no matter what. We refused to allow more dragons to die. So, we had a choice. We could save the dragons and rid the realm of all humans, turning us into the monsters the mortals claimed we were. Or…we could send the dragons away."

Shock reverberated through Esha as her head swiveled to him. Her lips formed the word *no*, but she already knew the answer.

"We gathered all our magic and opened a bridge into the cosmos." Kendrick's face creased with agony. "I've never felt anything so horrible as the pain of watching my clan leave. Worse, we had no idea where we were sending them. We hoped they found a place to call their own. Their chances were better than remaining on Earth. Once all the dragons were gone, we Kings returned to our central location, created a barrier that would keep humans out, and slept away centuries, waiting until they forgot we existed."

Esha swallowed past the lump in her throat. "Did they?"

"Aye. We live alongside them now, but we hide who we really are."

She wiped away the tears that streaked her face. "Your dragons found a home, though."

"We only recently discovered Zora. Eons of time have passed since we sent them away."

Which explained why he'd said that being a King was complicated. Esha guided him toward an incline of earth where they could stop for a bit. She waited until they reached it before turning to him. "Now that you've found the dragons, will you take them back to Earth?"

"That can never happen."

"Are you staying here then?"

He snorted and shrugged. "Another question I can no' answer. I think some of us would like to, but we're Earth's protectors. We can no' leave it undefended."

"It's fortunate that you found this realm for the dragons."

Kendrick's wince was visible. "We didna. A goddess named Erith had befriended Con. She's the one who created this realm in the image of ours to give the dragons a home."

"Created?" Esha choked.

"Aye."

Then Esha recalled who he'd said had done it. "A goddess?"

He gave her a small smile. "It's a lot to take in."

"You could say that." She'd discovered that shapeshifters were real, that Kendrick wasn't from this realm, and now that a goddess had created Zora. "Is Erith responsible for the infants who arrive here?"

"We asked her. She had no idea that happened."

Esha pointed to a mound of rock rising from the jungle. She moved into the shade the raised ground gave her and sat.

"The twins, Eurwen and Brandr, are the children of Constantine and his mate, Rhi, who is a Fae. They knew what happened on our realm, and they made sure that no one would encroach on the land of the dragons here."

"I don't blame the twins after what you told me."

Kendrick leaned back against the rocky hill. "Do elves fear dragons?"

Esha started to answer when the shadows near Kendrick began to move, and a Dark Elf emerged. In an instant, she dove into a roll and came up on her feet, her sword drawn, and the blade pressed against the Dark's throat. The elf glared at her with yellow eyes but didn't move.

"Kendrick," the Dark said through clenched teeth.

Shock went through Esha. "Kendrick, you know this Dark?"

"*Know* isna the word I'd use," Kendrick answered.

The Dark grunted. "I beg to differ."

"I warned you about the Dark," Esha told Kendrick.

Kendrick moved to stand beside her. "You told me they were harsh but no' evil."

Damn him for pointing that out. She didn't take her gaze from the Dark. "What does this one want with you?"

"Perhaps we should ask Dain," Kendrick said.

The Dark's yellow eyes narrowed on Kendrick. "Nice of you to point that out."

Everything in Esha told her not to trust the scarred elf. She didn't like that he already appeared to know Kendrick. Had everything Kendrick told her been a lie? When had the two met? Then she remembered that Kendrick had been alone during the night, giving the Dark an opportunity to approach.

"I don't trust Darks," she stated.

Yellow eyes met hers. "I don't trust you either."

"Esha." Kendrick called her name softly. "Let's hear Dain out."

She lowered her blade but didn't sheathe the weapon. Dain touched his neck where her sword had been and checked to see if she'd nicked his skin. His nostrils flared when he met her eyes again.

"What is it?" Kendrick asked the Dark.

Dain swung his head to Kendrick. "We need to leave. Now."

"Why?" Esha demanded, but Dain was already forming shadows. "We're not going anywhere until you explain yourself."

Dain didn't look at her, however. His yellow gaze stayed directed at Kendrick. "I told you last night that not everything is as it seems. There's more at work here than you know."

"Explain," Kendrick urged him.

Dain's lips thinned as he pressed them together. "There isn't time."

"Make time." Kendrick crossed his arms over his chest and waited.

Esha glanced around. She didn't see or sense any threats, but it was clear that Dain thought there were.

"The Conclave."

Kendrick looked at Esha. "The who?"

Esha blinked, confused as she looked at Kendrick. "The Conclave is a delegation of elves from Rannora and Belanore, as well as cities from beneath the water, ground, and in the mountains. They're elected officials who make sure we live peacefully."

"They've learned a Dragon King is here," Dain said.

Kendrick shrugged. "Let them come after me."

"It isn't you they want."

As the Dark said the last words, his gaze landed on her. Esha let the full impact of his statement fill her, but even then, she couldn't imagine what the Conclave would do to her.

"Can you get us somewhere safe?" Kendrick asked.

Dain gave him a flat look. "Would I have come if I couldn't?"

"No," Esha said and jerked away when Kendrick reached for her. "This Dark could be in on it."

Dain shrugged and stepped back into the moving shadows as his gaze moved past them. "Suit yourself."

"I think we should go with him," Kendrick said.

Esha gaped at him as he moved to stand with the Dark. When she saw that he also looked in the direction the Dark had, Esha glanced behind her. She saw nothing, but the ground trembled beneath her feet. The jungle erupted with the sounds of fleeing animals before it went deathly quiet. Something was headed toward them.

She looked at Kendrick and Dain. The idea of trusting the Dark was repulsive, but more than that, she knew she couldn't go belowground. Just thinking about it made her feel as if she couldn't breathe.

"Esha," Kendrick beseeched as he held out his hand.

She stared into his green eyes. He was calm while she was anything but. She knew better than to put her life in a Dark's hands, but she wasn't fool enough to stand on her own against whatever was coming.

"Make your decision," Dain told her. "Because I'm not waiting much longer."

Kendrick shot him a dark look before sliding his green gaze to her once more.

To hide the panic that grew exponentially, Esha stalked to them and said, "Do anything I deem deceitful, and I'll cut you in two."

"You're welcome to try, Sun Elf," Dain replied coolly before the shadows surrounded them.

Chapter Thirteen

Kendrick instinctively wrapped a protective arm around Esha as the world darkened with the shadows. It was so dense that he could see nothing past the thick darkness. No one moved for another two heartbeats, and then the darkness retreated. Kendrick looked around the unlit cavern, though it wasn't completely dark. The rocks themselves seemed to emit a pale blue glow to give light.

When he felt Esha trembling against him, he shifted his focus to her. Her breathing came in quick, harsh breaths. It hadn't entered his mind that she might be afraid of being underground, but she'd probably never had any reason to enter the Darks' domain before now.

"Where are we?" she demanded in a hoarse voice.

Dain went to the arched entryway and peered out. "I'd advise you both to keep your voices lowered. There are things in the deep you don't want to awaken."

"The deep?" Esha asked in a shaky voice.

Kendrick held her tighter, offering what comfort he could. She remained next to him as she struggled with the fear that clearly had her firmly in its grip.

Dain looked one way and then the other. He faced Kendrick. "No one knows about this place but me. It's a short walk to where we need to go."

"And where is that?" Kendrick asked.

Dain chuckled. "Don't worry, Dragon King. I'm not going to kill you."

"It's better if you doona try."

Dain's smile grew. "Then again, there is always tomorrow."

"I'm game whenever you are."

"I do think you are," the elf said, his yellow eyes twinkling.

The fact that Esha hadn't joined the banter reminded Kendrick that he needed to get her back into the sunlight. Despite the circumstances, he liked having her against him. Ever since she had looked at him with such hunger in her eyes that morning, he'd been hard-pressed not to think about what it would feel like to hold her. He'd worried that sex was off-limits for the Rangers, and he had been delighted to learn that the opposite was true.

Dain jerked his chin to Esha. "It might be better if she were unconscious."

"She'll be fine," Kendrick replied.

Dain shrugged. "Suit yourself. We need to move fast and quietly."

"How far down are we?"

"I don't think you really want to know."

Kendrick looked at the ceiling of rock above him. There wouldn't be enough room for him to shift here, but he wouldn't hesitate to do it if the need arose.

"I can tell what you're thinking. And as much as I'd like to see your true form, please don't. At least, not here."

Kendrick lowered his gaze to Dain and nodded. "Doona give me a reason."

"I'm helping, aren't I?"

"It appears that way."

Dain chuckled and turned, motioning for him to follow. Kendrick guided Esha. Her gaze darted about, and the rapidness of her breathing had him worried that she was about to hyperventilate. He ducked his head close to hers and said, "We'll be out quickly. Focus on your breathing. Slow it down."

She nodded, telling him she'd been listening all along.

They emerged from the cavern and walked along a wide tunnel that opened to an even larger area with ceilings that soared overhead. The blue glow was quite beautiful as it shone around them. Thick, towering columns dotted the area. As they passed one, Kendrick saw that some type of hieroglyphics covered the pillars.

Dain's strides were long and quick. He never slowed, and he never spoke. They kept pace with him while both Kendrick and Esha took in as much as they could. Everywhere he looked, that same blue glow came from the rocks. Was it from the Dark Elves' magic, or did it have something to do with the formation of the rocks themselves? It was something Kendrick hoped to learn.

Dain slowed his steps when they came to a long, narrow bridge. The elf paused and looked at Kendrick before briefly moving his gaze to Esha. Kendrick glanced over the edge of the bridge to see nothing but the soft glow that faded to black the deeper it went.

"Stay in the middle," Dain whispered.

Kendrick was about to comment that it was the only option since the walkway was so tight but nodded instead. Dain went first. He easily walked across the constricted passage. Kendrick urged Esha to follow. She faltered for only a moment before putting a foot on the bridge and starting across. Kendrick was close behind her. She was sure-footed, but they were still belowground, and he could tell she still battled her fear. But they all made it across without incident.

"This way," Dain whispered as he turned left.

He led them into a slender tunnel. Kendrick gave Esha credit. She didn't balk or turn away. She faced her fear, and he knew how much that likely took for her to do.

"It's not far now," the Dark explained.

Kendrick glanced behind him. "How deep was that back there?"

"Miles and miles," Dain answered.

"Did your people build all of this?"

Dain exited the passageway and waited for them. "Yes. There are tunnels that lead everywhere."

Kendrick didn't get a chance to ask more as shadows enveloped them. A second later, they were aboveground once more. Esha drew in a deep breath and bent at the waist, her hands on her knees. Kendrick fisted the hand that had held her, fighting against the need to reach for her so their fingers could intertwine.

Instead, he looked skyward and saw that it was twilight. A thick undergrowth of plants carpeted the forest floor as huge boulders dotted the area around them. In the distance, he heard the roar of water.

"What was after us?" Kendrick asked.

Dain shrugged, sweat covering his face. He weaved slightly as if he had overexerted himself. "I don't know."

"But you knew something was coming. How?"

"I have my ways."

Kendrick wasn't giving up that easily. "Earlier, you hinted that whatever was coming wasn't after me but Esha. Why?"

"I was hoping she'd know."

"I don't know anything," Esha said. She remained a few steps away, her back to them.

Kendrick glanced at her before returning his attention to Dain. "Why did you help us?"

"I overheard your tale earlier—at least, the ending. I'm sorry for what happened."

Kendrick bowed his head in acknowledgement. "That's why you intervened?"

"No."

"How long were you eavesdropping?"

"Not as long as you think."

"But you *were* following us?"

Dain shrugged. "I learned that you two were looking for the concealed creature that's been killing elves. I plan to join you."

Esha snorted. "No, thank you."

Kendrick didn't look away from Dain. For just a moment, the Dark Elf lowered the indifferent mask he showed to the world. "Who did the entity take from you?"

Dain was silent for so long that Kendrick didn't think he would answer. Then the Dark said, "A young elf I had taken under my wing."

Kendrick suspected that Dain didn't allow anyone close, but he clearly had with the child. And their death had struck the elf particularly hard.

"I'm going to find it," Dain declared.

The Dark allowed Kendrick to see the full extent of his pain and anguish. It went deep, marking Dain's soul in ways that he might never recover from. Kendrick knew that kind of agony. He and the other Kings had lived with it for too many years after losing the dragons and their freedom on Earth.

Just like that, Dain slid his mask back into place.

"You have connections that get you information, don't you?" Esha asked as she straightened and walked to them.

Kendrick inwardly smiled. He had hoped she had been listening and watching.

"I do," Dain answered.

Esha nodded. "That could come in handy. Right now, I want to know why the Conclave is targeting me."

"That could take some time," Dain began.

Kendrick exchanged a look with Esha before asking Dain, "What do you know about the thing we hunt?"

"It doesn't just strike aboveground," Dain replied.

That's what Kendrick had thought. "What about the Sea Elves?"

"They've been attacked, too."

Esha shook her head in disbelief. "Can no one see it?"

"No one," Dain answered.

"What about our magic?" Esha countered.

Dain shrugged one shoulder. "Maybe it would help if we could see it, but it strikes fast."

"We, too, have had difficulty," Kendrick admitted. "It'd be nice to know if it's just one entity or if there are more."

"It's just one," Dain said.

Esha's expression grew hard. "How do you know that?"

"I hear things."

Kendrick studied the Dark Elf. "What things?"

"There are rumors that someone called it here."

Esha's voice rose as she asked, "What?"

Dain held up his hands. "You asked, and I told you what I've heard. Right now, it's only a rumor."

"Or the truth," Kendrick said.

Esha put her hands on her hips and stared at Dain. "What have you heard about me?"

"That you're one of the best Rangers, if a bit reckless at times." Dain looked at Kendrick. "Like agreeing to work with a Dragon King."

Esha sighed loudly. "Things have been the same for too long. Isn't finding new allies better for everyone?"

"Some don't want change. Of any kind."

Esha snorted loudly. "The Conclave, you mean."

Kendrick frowned. "I thought they were elected."

"Some have held their positions for quite some time," Dain explained.

Kendrick nodded, thinking of some of the politicians on Earth who didn't have terms for their offices, allowing them to stay as long as they were elected again.

"They all have agendas," Esha said.

Dain nodded as he crossed his arms. "Those who have held their seats the longest have the most power."

"And the most to lose," Kendrick added.

"Why are they afraid of a King being here?" Esha asked.

Kendrick drew in a breath and slowly released it. "My guess is that there is something they doona want anyone to learn."

Chapter Fourteen

Esha didn't want to believe any of it, but too much was lining up. She wanted to go to her sister and demand that Savita ask the runes about the Conclave and everything else, but that wouldn't happen until she returned to Flamefall.

Two more days. That's all she had with Kendrick.

"There has to be more the Conclave wants Esha for than agreeing to hunt with me," he said.

Dain drew in a breath, his shoulders lifting as he did. "It could be her skills as a warrior."

"They would've sought me out before now," she said.

Kendrick asked, "Could it involve Savita?"

Esha's stomach clenched as she recalled the runes warning her sister of danger. Had Savita been trying to tell Esha that she was in danger? Or had the runes been telling Savita that *she* was the one in danger?

"It's well known that Savita is with Esha's Rangers. It's highly unusual for family members to be in the same camp," Dain explained.

Esha met his yellow eyes. "You know Savita?"

"Don't you know all the Readers?" he replied.

"Why would I?"

Dain snorted. "Readers hold incredible power both politically and magically, simply by their gift of reading the runes. It's said that any of them could take out the Conclave if they wanted."

"Maybe that's what this is all about," Kendrick said. "Perhaps the Conclave believes Savita is trying just that."

Esha was appalled that they would believe that. "My sister would never."

"Someone is doing something. The proof is you being targeted,"

Dain said.

Kendrick caught her gaze. "Has anything happened recently that would put you on the Conclave's radar?"

"No."

"What about Savita?"

Esha shook her head. "I'm not privy to everything my sister does, though." Then a realization hit her. "Do you think Flamefall was attacked? Could whatever came for me have gone for Savita first?"

"Or after," Kendrick added.

Dain's lips flattened as he shrugged. "It's possible, but moving against a Reader is unheard of. With one word, a Reader could have someone stripped of their power."

"Savita did say that the runes repeatedly warned her about danger," Kendrick said.

Dain's yellow eyes narrowed. "They did?"

Esha sighed, suddenly exhausted. "Yes. I've never seen her so shaken. She tried to determine who was at risk or what the threat was, but the runes wouldn't give her more information."

"Let me see if I can discern anything more," Dain told them as shadows closed around him.

Kendrick stepped forward. "Wait."

Dain paused the shadows and snapped, "What?"

"Are you recovered from earlier?"

The Dark looked slightly embarrassed at the question. "Using the shadows to travel takes…effort. The more I take with me, the more strain there is."

Esha hadn't even noticed that Dain clearly felt the effects of taking them across the distance. She knew better than to disregard things. She needed to do better.

"Watch yourself," Kendrick told Dain and stepped back.

Dain said nothing before vanishing.

Esha stared at Kendrick. "You like him."

"He has his moments," Kendrick said with a grin.

She couldn't return it. "I thought the only thing wrong was that something was killing elves. How could I not see that there was more?"

"You're out here doing your duty. How could you possibly know what politicians are doing or planning?"

"And my sister?"

Kendrick paused. "You know her. What do you think?"

"I think she became someone else when she became a Reader. She was always bossy, but ever since you arrived, she's acted strangely. I thought it was merely because I overstepped. Now, I'm not so sure."

"Do you have any way of contacting her?"

"I can, but it would give away our location."

He glanced around at the thick forest around them. "And where are we?"

"On the other side of the river. Dain took us a significant distance."

"I still think I'm the one they were after earlier."

Esha shrugged and wrinkled her nose. "Whether it's you or me, if we're together, does it matter?"

"Nay," he said after a brief pause.

She cleared her throat. "This looks like a good area to rest for the night."

"Are there any Wood Elves near? I'd rather no' run across anyone else until we get more answers."

Esha climbed onto one of the massive boulders and tried to get her bearings. She heard the distant rumble of the river to her left. She and her squad had been this way before, but it had been some time. She jumped to the ground. "They already know we're here. If they want to interact with us, they'll come regardless."

Kendrick's lips quirked in a grin. "In that case, we rest."

She wasn't sure she could. Pent-up energy churned through her, and it needed a release. Unfortunately, her mind was too jumbled with questions and unease, and all she could do was stand there. She had no idea how long she remained before she smelled food. Her stomach rumbled, reminding her that she hadn't eaten much that day.

Esha found Kendrick before a fire, roasting what looked like a bird. "What's that?"

"We call it chicken. I decided to improvise." He tore off a leg and handed it to her.

She sniffed it before taking a bite. There was no gamey flavor, which surprised her. "Not bad."

"Have as much as you'd like. I've already eaten my fill. I asked you earlier if you were hungry, but you were too deep in your thoughts."

"I'm sorry," she said as she sat beside him.

"My thoughts are also full."

They fell into a comfortable silence as she ate her meal. Esha kept trying to form a plan, but it was nearly impossible to do when she didn't know what might come for them. And sitting next to Kendrick, it was impossible to ignore him. She wasn't surprised by her attraction. He was a

Dragon King, after all. But the more she learned about him, the more his allure became less about lust and more about…something else.

She thought about him in the water and the visceral reaction of her body to seeing him. She thought of being underground and how he had wrapped an arm around her. Holding on to him had gotten her through her time in the dark without completely losing control of herself. The feelings he stirred within her were dangerous. Every Ranger was warned to stay away from anyone who caused such emotions.

And yet, she was alone with him.

Esha shook herself. Whatever this thing was with Kendrick was new and exciting, but she needed to keep her sights on the future she wanted. He would be gone in a few days. Did she really want to destroy everything she had worked so hard for? It was better to remove herself from anyone who tempted her in such a way. She got to her feet and started walking away when she saw the two tents. They were smaller than Kendrick's previous one but still round.

"Take your pick," he told her with a smile.

She chose the one on the right. The bed was decent-sized, but she barely noticed. She paced the confines of the enclosure as she repeatedly tried to get her mind to rest. But she couldn't stop thinking about Kendrick.

Esha closed her eyes and tried to center herself. Emotions used to rule her as a child. Ranger training had taught her how to control the feelings that got away from her—like now. She slowed her breathing and imagined the rays of the sun warming her. Little by little, the strong emotions began to ebb, as all things did.

When she felt like herself again, she opened her eyes and took a good look around the shelter. Besides the bed, there was a chair and a small table. Tiny lights ringed the inside of the tent, casting a soft glow. Esha sat on the bed and grinned as she sank into the softness. She lay back and stared up at the top of the round lodging.

She heard Kendrick moving around outside. She could picture him tending to the fire, his muscles stretching and bunching beneath his shirt. If she were in his place, she would've returned to her people, but he remained, even as the threats intensified.

Savita had said that Esha had three days with Kendrick. The first day had passed quickly and without much tracking. Three days wasn't enough time to do anything. Esha bit the inside of her lip as she contemplated what might happen if she took longer. Would Savita cover for her?

Regardless, the entity killing elves and dragons needed to be stopped.

If Esha took that stand, it could cost her her position. But lives would be saved—not just elves but dragons, too. She thought about what she would say to anyone who questioned her decisions. Would anyone believe she had been targeted? What about Kendrick? Others would likely think he had been the focus, but would they care? It was doubtful. Of course, she was contemplating all of this on the word of a Dark.

Esha wanted to hate Dain and all he'd said, but too much of it made sense. Too many things caused her to question everything. And *that* was why she would continue hunting the foe.

As for Savita, her sister was resourceful. The Reader could take care of herself—she always had. The real concern was whether Esha could complete this mission. Kendrick could leave anytime he wanted. Dain, however, would face the same wrath from the Conclave that Esha did.

If they were caught.

The sound of Kendrick moving in his tent halted her thoughts. She wondered if he was getting undressed. She could picture him bending over to tug off his boots, causing the material of his shirt to stretch tightly over his back and shoulders. He would likely stand and yank his shirt from his trousers before grabbing the hem and pulling it over his head. Would he toss it aside or fold it? She imagined he would fold it because he seemed the meticulous type. Then, he would unbutton his pants and push them down before stepping out of them. Of course, he'd fold them to lie next to his shirt.

She heard a splash of water. She turned her head toward his tent, wishing she could see through the material. Was he washing his face? Esha smiled as she thought about seeing the beaded droplets traveling down his hard body as she had that morning.

She bit her lip as her body heated. Her sex clenched with need. The object of her desire was so close. All she had to do was walk over.

If she did, she would be crossing a line she'd sworn never to cross.

Esha pushed to her feet and made her way to the side of her tent nearest to Kendrick's. She placed her hand on the thick, rough fabric. She closed her eyes and sought to center herself again, but nothing worked.

There was only one thing she wanted.

Chapter Fifteen

Kendrick paced and then sat before pacing some more. Esha had been withdrawn all evening. He wished he'd found some words to ease her concern, but that was more Merrill's department. His friend always had a pep talk at the ready and somehow always knew what to say. Kendrick didn't have that gift, and this was the first time he wished he did.

Seeing Esha so troubled bothered him. Mainly because he liked her. A lot. He appreciated her cleverness, her wit, and her loyalty—not to mention her dedication to her people. She knew her strengths and how to use them, but she also knew her weaknesses and had learned how to work around them. To top it off, she was, hands down, the most exquisite being he had ever seen.

He remembered the moment of fear in her eyes when he shifted, but it hadn't lasted long. Since then, she had been open and friendly. He had looked close for any deception in her words or actions, but he had found none. Her demeanor and voice had held empathy when he told her about his history. And while he might have only briefly seen her fight, she had been magnificent. If a King couldn't be there to aid him, he couldn't imagine anyone else by his side.

It was no wonder he liked her.

As for the pull he felt toward her...he didn't deny it, nor had he stopped thinking about what her lips might taste like. But he wouldn't act on it—even after seeing desire sparking in her eyes that morning. The Rangers might not be celibate, but he wasn't a one-night-stand kind of lover. He liked to take his time and get to know his partners. And that could take weeks or months. And with Esha, he knew he would want it all.

If there were even a chance of that, he wouldn't hesitate to woo her.

To turn on all his charm and seduce her, little by little. He knew they would be good together. She clearly felt their attraction. Her look that morning had said as much.

Perhaps he was being too hasty in disregarding it. Why *not* take a single night? Their attraction was strong—very strong. Kendrick couldn't remember feeling something quite so acutely before. The more he was around her, the more he heard her voice, saw her smile, and looked into her golden-amber eyes, the more his yearning to know her—body and soul—grew.

Just thinking about Esha made heat flood his body now. His fingers ached to have her in his hold. His hands tingled as he remembered holding her lithe form earlier underground. He recalled how she had fit perfectly against him, how she had gripped him as if he were the only thing keeping her standing. It was the most vulnerable he'd seen her—a proud warrior elf who had battled her darkest fears. He wanted to make sure she never felt that way again. He sought to be the one to protect her. An elf who didn't need his—or anyone's—protection.

But, still, he wanted to be the one she turned to.

"Fuck," he murmured.

He walked to the table and used his magic to conjure a bowl of cold water. He wet his face, but what he really needed was an icy shower.

Kendrick stilled as he heard something outside. His enhanced senses instantly went on alert. He walked to the flap and lifted it to find Esha. In his present mood, this was the last place she should be.

"Can I come in?" she asked.

As if he would deny her. As if he *could*. He moved aside to allow her entry, his gaze following her. He noted her bare feet and her gorgeous, tawny locks that fell around her shoulders. His eyes lingered on her backside before she slowly turned to face him. There was something different in her gaze tonight. Something he couldn't quite name. "Is everything all right?"

"Everything's fine."

Something had changed about Esha, and he couldn't put his finger on what. He continued studying her as she walked to him. His breath hitched when she stopped mere inches before him. He couldn't breathe, couldn't think as he stared into her beautiful eyes. She gently placed her hands on his chest. Her lids lowered, and her lips parted slightly. He fisted his hands as she leaned forward and pressed her mouth to his. Shock went through him, followed by a poignant rush of desire. It engulfed him. He didn't move for fear she would change her mind and leave.

The kiss was brief. He bit back a groan as she leaned away. He opened his eyes and met her gaze. She smiled and licked her lips. That small movement was nearly his undoing. His body shook with the need to touch her, to pull her close and feel all her softness.

She leaned in for another kiss. Kendrick was prepared this time, but it didn't dull the sweet taste of her or the yearning that consumed him. He hesitantly put his hands on her hips as their mouths brushed. When he parted his lips and swept his tongue against hers, she sighed and wound her arms around his neck. Kendrick splayed a palm across her back to hold her as he tangled his other hand in her silken hair.

They exchanged no words as they deepened the kiss. Desire intensified, expanding as the flames of it licked recklessly between them. Their hunger grew until it pulsed in time with their hearts. His breaths were ragged, and his skin burned with need. The feel of her in his arms was almost too much, yet not nearly enough.

With one look, one kiss, he was hers. Completely.

He fumbled for the fastenings on her corset, yanking too hard in his bid to undo them. Their lips didn't break apart as she helped him unlatch the last of the buckles. The corset fell with a soft *thump* to the ground. He put his hands on her hips, searching the waist of her pants for fastenings. He found the buttons and quickly released them. Then, he pushed the material over her hips and shoved them down her legs.

Esha kicked her legs free. As soon as she did, Kendrick lifted her. She wrapped her legs around his waist. Her fingers sank into his hair, and she held his head as she kissed him deeply, passionately.

Her taste was as perfect and wonderful as he'd known it would be. He couldn't get enough of her kisses. If he did nothing else but kiss her for the rest of eternity, it would be enough. But she offered so much more, and he wasn't about to pass it up.

Kendrick walked to the bed. She unhooked her legs so he could lower her to the mattress. Esha shifted to her knees and yanked at his shirt. He broke the kiss long enough to tug it over his head. Then, their lips tangled again. Her skin was soft and smooth, and the cool locks of her hair slid over the backs of his hands, teasing him.

When her hands covered his arousal through his pants, he groaned. He couldn't wait to be inside her, to feel her wet heat surrounding him as he pumped. Kendrick yanked at the button of his pants so hard that it flew off. Esha ended the kiss and watched as he removed his trousers.

Her gaze lowered to his hard cock that jutted between them. She licked her lips, making his balls tighten. It had been so very long since anyone had made him *burn*. Her beautiful eyes lifted to his face. She grabbed the hem of her shirt and pulled it over her head. His eyes fastened on her breasts. She slid from the bed and tugged the undergarment down her hips.

When she straightened, she stood naked before him. Her brown skin shimmered golden and stretched over her toned body. Kendrick was utterly awed by her beauty, staggered by the longing reflected in her eyes.

Shaken by the depths of his hunger.

He eyed her small, pert breasts that rose and fell quickly with her breaths. He took in the hard, dark nipples that begged for his lips. His hands itched to learn the curve of her waist and the flare of her hips. To travel over her taut stomach. A small patch of tawny curls sat at the junction of her thighs. And her legs... He couldn't wait to feel them wrapped around him again as he sank into her.

* * * *

Never in her life had Esha thought she would find herself standing on the precipice of such a monumental act. She had known what she wanted—and what would happen—the moment she walked to Kendrick's tent. She also knew the outcome.

And she didn't care.

How could she when she knew this moment of her standing naked with a Dragon King was meant to be? The realization had come to her quickly and with as much certainty as when she realized she would be a Ranger.

Kendrick's kisses were intoxicating, his touch thrilling. Right now, in this moment, she didn't care what happened. She wanted to hold on to these amazing feelings inside her and share the night with this Dragon King.

Her skin warmed as his gaze roamed over her. He wasn't the only one staring, however. She couldn't look away from his hard body. She had seen his chest that morning, and she couldn't get enough of it. His light skin held no scars, but she knew he had some deep within him that no one saw. She felt them, though. Just as she had felt his strength when she leaned against him underground.

Esha's breath hitched when her gaze traveled down the V-shape of his chest to his hips and took in the sight of his impressive arousal once again. Her sex clenched in need as she imagined him sliding inside her. His thick legs were corded with more muscles and dusted with dark hair.

They reached for each other at the same time. Esha put her hands on his stomach and let her palms caress upward, running over the muscles of his chest to his neck. His hands gripped her hips, holding her tightly against him, his cock between them.

Then they were kissing again. Esha let herself become lost in the desire. She gave herself over to the intense and heady passion that governed her. Kendrick leaned her slowly backward until she lay on the bed and then settled on top of her. She sighed at the feel of his weight. Her legs parted and wrapped around him.

He kissed across her jaw and down her neck. He paused and licked the divot where her collarbones met before moving lower, leaving a trail of hot kisses across her skin. Her breaths came faster as he neared her breast. Then his lips wrapped around a peak and gave a slight pull before he moved his tongue around it.

Esha arched her back, losing herself to the delicious feel. Pleasure ran from her nipples straight to her sex. She ground her hips into him, wanting more. And he gave it to her. He continued suckling, making her mindless with growing need. When she didn't think she could take any more, he moved to her other breast. Her fingers dug into his back as the yearning for an orgasm consumed her. She teetered on the edge, ready at any moment.

A cry of pleasure ripped from her when he slipped a finger inside her. He moved it in time with his tongue on her nipple.

"Yes," she cried out hoarsely.

This was what she needed. She gripped his hand, trying to get him to move it faster, but he ignored her. Didn't he realize how close she was? Didn't he understand how much she needed the release? A sob locked in her throat as he kept to the same tempo.

"Please," she begged.

In response, his thumb circled her clit. Esha jerked at the sensation and waited for more. Instead, Kendrick settled between her thighs. His green eyes briefly met hers before he lowered his mouth to her sex.

Her breath locked in her lungs when his tongue swept over her. If she'd thought his fingers had felt good, it was nothing compared to his tongue. It became impossible for her to move. She was caught within a compelling web of potent pleasure. Her flushed body buzzed with need, every nerve ending firing with ecstasy.

It was the most wonderful thing she had ever experienced.

His tongue quickened as he ruthlessly teased her swollen clit. Desire tightened low in her belly, bringing her closer and closer to climax. She sought it, reached for it. When the orgasm hit, for just an instant, she felt as if she were suspended in time. In the next heartbeat, waves of bliss rolled through her, one on top of the other until she couldn't catch her breath.

* * * *

She was magnificent, unreservedly spectacular. Kendrick watched Esha as she climaxed, tasting her on his tongue. He knew then that he had made a fatal error. Once would never be enough for him. He had known with their first kiss, but he hadn't admitted it until that moment. Esha was his mate.

He put that out of his mind for the moment because he didn't want to think of the issues that presented. Instead, he focused on her. He continued licking her, prolonging her orgasm for as long as he could. When her body began to relax, he rose and guided his cock to her entrance. He looked at her to find her eyes open and locked on him. Kendrick gently rubbed the head of his cock against her folds.

She moaned and jerked in response. Then she opened her legs wider and tugged him toward her. He found her entrance and pushed inside her tight, slick walls. He pulled out slightly and thrust deep.

Her groan matched his. He stayed still for a moment, taking it all in. As he gazed into her eyes, her lips curved into a smile before she locked her legs around his waist and moved slightly so he slid deeper. Kendrick closed his eyes. He hadn't even begun to thrust yet, and already, he was about to spill his seed.

When he did start pumping his hips, she met him thrust for thrust. Each time, he found himself sinking deeper and deeper into the pleasure until he couldn't tell where he ended and she began. Their sweat-slicked bodies glided against each other, the delicious friction propelling him faster toward climax.

Her nails sank into his skin as she jerked beneath him. He saw the ecstasy fill her face as her body clamped around his cock. Kendrick pumped his hips harder, faster. With a shout, he buried himself deep within her as he orgasmed.

For long moments, neither of them moved. Esha pulled him down atop her and held him in her arms. He buried his face against her neck and wished he could stop time so the night would never end. But he didn't have that power. He rose on his hands and gave her a quick kiss before pulling out of her and rolling onto his back. Kendrick extended his arm and waited. Esha turned to her side and curled against him.

"We're going to do that again tonight," she said.

He laughed. "I was just thinking the same thing."

"I've never felt anything so…"

"Me, either."

She shifted her head to look at him. Her lips parted, but no words came out. Then she looked away. Kendrick tightened his arm around her. Clearly, neither wanted to talk about what would happen in the morning. For now, they would stay in the moment.

Chapter Sixteen

She should be resting, but it was the last thing Esha wanted to do. Her body hummed with contentment the likes of which she had never experienced. She'd had good sex before, but nothing compared to what she'd just shared with Kendrick. Everything had felt…right.

The sound of rain hitting the tent filled the silence between them. It was nice just lying with him. She could hear his heartbeat beneath her ear, and his fingers lazily traced designs on her back.

"What do these mean?" he asked as his other hand lightly touched one of her face markings.

"The forehead marking is that of a sun. The dots along my brows were a design I chose that signifies family. The lines on my cheeks represent my warrior nature."

"They're beautiful."

She smiled as she rose on an elbow to look down at him. "Really?"

His eyes crinkled at the corners as he grinned. "Aye, lass."

By the sun, how she loved when he called her that. His deep voice was the most beautiful sound she had ever heard. And the way he spoke with his accent was particularly pleasing. "Do your people mark yourselves in any way?"

"We call them tattoos."

"Do you have any?" She had seen him from the front, but there was always a chance he had one elsewhere.

His lips widened in a grin. "Aye."

Kendrick sat and turned his back to her. Esha's lips parted in shock at the image of the dragon covering his back. She couldn't tell if the ink was black or red, and she finally gave up trying to decide. The design itself was so intricate that she couldn't imagine how much time it had taken or even how it had been done. The dragon stood, showing its left side. Its wings were spread wide and slightly upward, its tail curled as it lay behind it, and its front left foot was lifted as if it were about to take a step. But it was the dragon's stare that caught her. It appeared as if it were looking right at her.

"I've never seen anything like it," she murmured and ran her fingers over the tattoo. "It's beautiful."

Kendrick turned his head to the side to look at her. "Every King has one. Each is different. We've always wondered if dragons have them, too, but until we shifted, we did no' know about them."

"Because your scales would cover it?"

"Aye."

"It's a shame that it's covered all the time. This should be displayed."

He returned to his back and grinned up at her. "Are you suggesting I walk around shirtless?"

"I'm saying I wouldn't mind," she answered with a smile.

He laughed and pulled her back down beside him. "Shall I try it tomorrow?"

"With the rain, it won't matter what you wear because you'll be soaked regardless."

"Verra true."

Esha debated whether to meditate. Elves didn't need to sleep like humans, but they did require four hours of meditation each night. But the thought of wasting what little time she had with Kendrick felt wrong. She wrapped her fingers around his flaccid cock and began stroking him.

"Lass," he murmured in a deep, throaty voice.

"Would you rather sleep?"

He groaned when she cupped his balls. "Absolutely no'."

"I didn't think so."

He hardened in her hand. She ran her fingers around the head of his arousal, causing a groan to rumble from his chest. His eyes blazed with desire, and his breathing grew harsh. He had held her immobile as he brought her to the brink earlier. She wanted to do the same for him, but she already craved him inside her again. She wasn't sure she could hold out for as long as he had.

Esha straddled his hips and hovered over him. His hands smoothed up her thighs, his thumbs grazing her still-sensitive clit before moving up her stomach. Her breathing had quickened, her blood rushing through her quickly. Just a look, a simple touch from him, had her quivering.

His large hands held her softly. She reached down and took his cock once more, holding it as she slowly lowered herself onto him. When he was nestled within her, she began leisurely rocking her hips back and forth.

His eyes burned with need. She couldn't look away from him, even when he palmed both breasts and massaged them. Even when he thumbed her nipples and made her want to grind against him. He held her gaze as he kept one hand rolling a nipple between his fingers and his other lowered to rub her clit.

The pleasure that rushed through her was simply too much. She rocked her hips faster, eager to experience another orgasm—and to feel him spill inside her.

They were breathing hard, their moans filling the tent. With him thrusting deep, his finger teasing her clit and her nipple, she reached climax in record time. Esha gasped, her breath locked in her lungs as her body jerked from the ecstasy.

In an instant, Kendrick was behind her, and she was on her hands and knees. He thrust into her, powerfully and deep. She cried out as a second orgasm came, layering on top of the first. He held her hips as he drove into her, hard and fast. She lost track of time, of herself. All she knew was amazing bliss. It covered her, inside and out.

Slowly, she came back to herself, her body still shuddering, when she felt Kendrick climax, his seed once more filling her. For the first time, Esha wondered what it would be like to have her belly swell with a child. It was wishful thinking, however. No one on the planet could conceive.

They fell to their sides together, too exhausted to move. A short while later, Kendrick pulled out of her and covered them with a blanket as he snuggled against her. It would be so easy to sleep, her body seemed to want that, but Esha refused to allow it.

"We do that rather nicely," he said as he kissed the back of her neck.

She smiled. "Hm. We certainly do."

"Are you hungry? We worked up an appetite."

She rolled over to look at him. "That we have."

Kendrick got to his feet and held out his hand. "Come, then."

Esha didn't hesitate to take his offered palm. He pulled her up. She left the blanket on the bed. As she came around to the front of the tent, a rug and pillows that hadn't been there before awaited them. They lowered themselves to the ground.

"What would you like?" he asked.

"More of your food."

"Are you adventurous?"

Esha couldn't help but laugh. "I'm a Ranger. Of course, I'm adventurous."

"That doesna always mean the same things when it comes to food."

"Surprise me," she told him.

He thought about that for a moment. "Do you want sweet or salty?"

"Sweet."

Kendrick flashed a smile as a plate appeared between them. "They doona look like much, but they're delicious."

She eyed the treats covered in white dust. "What are they?"

"They're called beignets. It's a dough that's fried and then covered in powdered sugar."

Esha watched as he lifted one of the pastries and bit into it. The sugar coated his lips and fell down his chest. She laughed at the delight that filled his face. He said nothing as he finished off the treat.

"Doona even try no' to get the sugar on you. It gets everywhere, but that's part of the appeal."

She grabbed a beignet and sniffed it.

"Do you smell everything?" he asked with a chuckle.

She shot him a flat look. "Don't you? If it doesn't smell good, I'm not going to eat it." But the treat smelled delicious. Esha took a small bite, surprised at the taste of the dough and sugar that filled her mouth.

"I knew you'd like them," Kendrick said with a smug smile.

She grinned and took another bite. One simply wasn't enough. It didn't take long for them to finish the plate of treats. When they finished, she looked down to find herself coated in the powdered sugar.

It took some time to get it off, especially when they helped each other by using their lips and tongues. He made her moan and then laugh before she did the same to him. Once they were reasonably clean, they reclined on the pillows. The night had been nothing like Esha had expected, but she wasn't sorry for it. Even when she knew what would come with the dawn.

"What's it like to have a family?" she asked.

He gently tugged on a piece of her hair and shrugged. "Some people have such horrible families they wish they didna have any."

"What about you?"

"Mine was fine. Nothing bad, nothing great. I didna have siblings. My parents spent a lot of time away. My father was in the army, and my mother was a high-ranking clan member. Her duties took her away frequently, too. I spent considerable time alone."

"But you know where you come from."

His green gaze slid to her. "Aye."

"That's what I've never had. None of us brought to Zora against our will have that. It's indescribable, that feeling of not knowing who your family is or where you come from. It's like a missing piece inside me."

Kendrick linked his fingers with hers. "You may no' know who your parents are or where you came from, but you know who *you* are. You found your calling as a Ranger. That's what matters. Some have a good, solid family and never find themselves."

"I'd still like to have answers. What if my parents didn't want me?"

He pulled her into his arms and kissed the top of her head. "They wanted you."

"You can't know that."

"I do, lass. Because I know you."

Chapter Seventeen

The night passed too quickly. Kendrick lamented the fact, but he could do nothing about it. Exhaustion took Esha, and he finally urged her to rest. It was interesting to learn that elves didn't need sleep, only meditation.

He remained with her on the pillows while she meditated, enjoying the simple pleasure of holding her. His mate. His heart panged at the realization. In his wildest dreams, he'd never thought to discover that his mate was on Zora and an elf.

He almost woke her several times to tell her that she was his fated mate, but he couldn't seem to get the words out. They were good together, but her life was with the Rangers. She had made that abundantly clear. Her position dictated that she not bind herself to anyone. He had known that when she'd come to him last night, but that had been before he'd known that she was his mate.

But how could he expect her to give up everything to be with him? What would he do in her shoes?

Kendrick thought about Con and the rest of the Kings. On Earth, the mates remained with the Kings on Dreagan, but Zora wasn't Earth. A precedent had already been set on this realm. Varek had found his mate with Jeyra. She'd chosen to be with Varek, and they lived with the dragons. They also traveled back and forth to Earth. It could be said that Jeyra's decision was easy since the people she trusted had been trying to harm Varek, but Kendrick didn't think anything was that black and white.

Then there was Cullen and Tamlyn. The Banshee hid with her three friends because they each had magic, and Cullen divided his time between Cairnkeep and the underground ruins of Iron Hall right outside the border.

The most recent pairing was Shaw and Nia. She had been a slave to the Divine at Stonemore, and Shaw had helped break Nia free. The two of them now lived at Cairnkeep—at least for the time being.

Kendrick needed to tell Esha that they were meant to be together. A Dragon King couldn't live without his mate. Would it be enough if Kendrick snuck into Shecrish to see her? Would she even agree since it would break her vow to the order? Could he put her in such a position? If he didn't, he would be dooming himself. He sighed, his heart heavy. She could leave the Rangers anytime she wanted, but she was a warrior at heart. She had found her place with them.

The night had been the most fulfilling and wonderful of his very, very long life. But the future looked bleak, at best. Until he spoke to Esha, all he could do was worry over the same things when he should be concentrating on their mission.

He heard a sound outside the tent. Kendrick slowly extricated himself from Esha. She didn't move as he quietly got to his feet and dressed. He pushed aside the tent's flap to reveal the gray light of dawn. Though the rain had stopped an hour earlier, water still dripped from the edges of the yurt. The magical fire he'd created continued to burn. When Kendrick glanced to the side, he spotted Dain.

The Dark Elf leaned against one of the boulders, his arms crossed over his chest as he stared at the shelter. Kendrick glanced back at Esha before exiting and walking to the elf. Dain pushed away from the rock and grinned.

"About time you two got together," Dain said.

Kendrick chose to ignore him. "What did you find out?"

"You didn't really think either of you was hiding the attraction from anyone, did you?"

Kendrick simply stared at the elf.

Dain threw up his hands. "I didn't see or hear anything. Is that better?"

"Much. Now, did you discover anything?"

The Dark Elf glanced at the tent and lowered his voice. "Yes."

Unease slithered through Kendrick. "What?"

"A lot's happening. Elves everywhere are on edge."

The flap to the yurt lifted, and Esha came out, buckling her corset. "What's going on?"

Kendrick stepped to the side so she could join them. "I was about to find out."

"As I was saying," Dain said, "the elves are troubled. They're sending out multiple calls for Rangers."

Her brows drew together. "Where?"

"Everywhere." Dain ran a hand down his face. "And I do mean everywhere. The calls are coming from the mountains, as well."

"That's never happened before," Esha said in an unsteady voice.

Kendrick looked between the two. He then turned to Dain. "Why? What's causing it?"

"I haven't gotten a definitive answer," the elf said.

But he knew *something*. Kendrick was sure of it. "Tell us what you've heard."

Dain glanced at Esha, unable to hold her gaze. "I should find out more."

"Tell us," Esha demanded.

The Dark visibly winced. "Understand that there could be any number of reasons."

"Dain," Kendrick warned.

"Your sister is missing," Dain told Esha.

Esha's face went slack. "What do you mean?"

"Just that." Dain blew out a breath. "It happened sometime after you left yesterday."

"How do you know this?" Kendrick asked.

Dain lifted a shoulder. "As I keep telling you, word spreads fast among the elves. A Reader doesn't just vanish like that. It has caused concern within every class."

"I should return to Flamefall. I need to find out what happened," Esha said.

Kendrick rubbed his chin. "Could she have been called away?"

"Yes," Esha replied reluctantly. "But, surely, she would've told someone."

"I think Flamefall is the last place you want to be," Dain said.

Kendrick swiveled his head to the elf, and that same troubled feeling returned. This time stronger. "Why?"

Dain shifted his weight from one foot to the other as he fought to hold their gazes. "I don't want to tell you because I've not confirmed anything yet."

"Confirmed what?" Esha asked, her gaze locked on the Dark.

Dain sighed loudly. "Remember my warning when we were underground to lower your voices?"

"You said there were things we shouldna wake," Kendrick said with a nod. "Are you telling us we woke something?"

"We didn't." Dain looked away hastily. "Someone else did."

Esha shrugged. "I'm sorry for your people, but what does that have to do with us?"

Kendrick understood Dain's expression, and his gut constricted painfully. "It's been let loose up here."

"Yes," Dain murmured.

Kendrick's heart seized as foreboding shivered through him. "What is it?"

"A nightwraith. It prefers the underground caverns, but it can—and will—hunt aboveground," Dain explained.

Esha nodded. "Tell us everything. We can hunt it."

Dain snorted loudly. "Don't you think we've done that? There's a reason some creatures are left alone. This is one we've learned to avoid at all costs. We've abandoned huge portions of cities when one gets too close."

"Why?" Kendrick pressed.

Dain briefly squeezed his eyes closed. "It's hard to kill. Even with magic. It's large enough that it considers us dinner. Its fangs are…enormous, and the venom is lethal with just one drop. There's no sneaking up on it. Its hearing is impeccable, and even taking out its eyes won't hinder it. It can even shoot toxic shards from its body. Once it locks on to you, there's no getting away from it."

"Is that what came for us yesterday?" Esha asked.

The Dark shrugged but looked away. "I think so."

"You knew we were in danger," Kendrick pressed. "I think you know more."

Dain swung his gaze to Kendrick and shook his head. "I'm telling you all I know. If I had known it was a nightwraith, I would've taken you much, much farther."

That got Kendrick's attention. He narrowed his gaze. "Why?"

"Once before, a Dark Elf used a nightwraith for revenge." Dain paused, his lips pursed as if just mentioning it was distasteful. "The elf left the scent of the one she wanted harmed behind when she disturbed the creature. The nightwraith latched on to that scent and sought out the victim over miles and weeks. That's how we learned there's no getting away from it, no matter how far you run or how cleverly you've hidden."

Kendrick's blood turned to ice. He glanced at Esha to see her lips parted in shock. His mind raced with options as he asked Dain, "Did you stop it?"

Dain shook his head slowly. "Hundreds of elves gathered and fought it with magic and weapons, but that only enraged the beast more. Over two hundred Dark were killed that day, including the one the nightwraith sought. Once its intended victim was dead, the creature turned on those around it until the elves retreated. Only then did it leave."

"Bloody hell," Kendrick murmured.

Esha lifted her chin. "Well, then. There's no point in running. And I'm not going to bring that beast into this forest to harm others. If it wants me, bring me back to where you first found us."

"Have you lost your mind?" Dain asked in disbelief.

Kendrick caught her gaze. There was no way he would let Esha near the creature. "Nay."

"You heard him," she stated as she motioned to Dain. "I can't outrun it, and I don't want innocents to die while it's hunting me."

Kendrick turned to look at the yurts. He used his magic to remove them, along with the fire, leaving no trace of them behind. Then he turned to Dain and Esha. "I'm no' giving up that easily. Are either of you?"

Dain snorted. "You say that because you've not faced a nightwraith."

"Neither have you," Kendrick pointed out.

"That doesn't mean I don't know how dangerous they are."

Esha turned to him. "What do you suggest?"

"We were already after a mutual foe. Is this really about you or me? Or is it about the entity?" Kendrick asked.

Dain leaned back against the bolder. "You can't be suggesting that someone is trying to stop you."

"Why not?" Esha shrugged. "It's a good theory. Savita might have limited our time together, but I think that was because of what I did to her. When I saw her the next morning, that was something different. She was deeply troubled."

Dain's white brows rose on his forehead. "And you still set out with Kendrick? Savita is a Reader. You should've listened to her."

"Can they no' lie?" Kendrick asked.

Dain frowned, affronted by the mere suggestion. "They don't."

"But they can," Esha said. "Nothing's stopping them. Everyone believes them because if we begin to doubt, then everything falls apart."

A muscle jumped in Dain's jaw. But he didn't disagree with Esha.

"Also, she never told me not to go," Esha added. "She *asked* me to stay. When I declined, she told me to be careful."

Kendrick shrugged one shoulder. "She cares about you. I doona think she would put you in danger."

"I don't think so either. There's no way Savita sent the nightwraith,"

Esha told them.

Kendrick hoped she was right. "Do you know where she could've gone?"

"She's supposed to remain in Flamefall. The only way she would leave is if a Ranger sent for her. Savita takes her station seriously."

"Or if she's called to the Reader Temple," Dain said.

Esha's nose wrinkled. "True. Though it isn't like her to leave without telling someone. No group of Rangers is left without a Reader. Ever."

"What if a Reader dies?" Kendrick asked.

Dain lifted one shoulder in a shrug. "The Readers stay far from any skirmishes. They're revered. Protected. At all costs."

"Even if one of them makes a decision that goes against someone?" Kendrick prodded.

It was Esha's turn to shrug. "It happens all the time. No one has attacked a Reader in dozens of generations."

That didn't mean it couldn't happen, just that it was unlikely. Kendrick still didn't understand the full role of a Reader. The way Esha and Dain spoke about them, no one made a decision without consulting them. Kendrick had met Esha's Rangers, and all of them appeared intelligent. Especially Esha. If she had gained the rank she had, why did Esha need a Reader to make military decisions?

"All right. If it isn't Savita, then who?" Kendrick looked from Esha to Dain.

Neither had an answer.

Chapter Eighteen

"We can't stay here," Esha said.

Dain pushed away from the boulder. "There's nowhere you can go that the nightwraith won't find you."

"Dragon land," Kendrick said.

Esha jerked her head to him. "You want us to cross into Idrias? We're not supposed to cross the boundary. You know that."

"These are extenuating circumstances."

"We don't know if it's after me or you. We're taking his word," she said, jabbing a finger at Dain.

The Dark glared at her. "I didn't have to help, and I'm beginning to think I shouldn't have."

"No one asked you to," she snapped.

Kendrick held up a hand. "There's no need to turn on each other. We're all in a predicament, and we need to trust each other when there's verra little to none between us."

Esha couldn't stop thinking about her sister. She was upset and afraid that something had happened to Savita. That caused her to lash out at Dain, which wasn't fair to the Dark. He *had* been helping.

She rubbed her forehead. Savita wouldn't just disappear. But where had she gone? Esha didn't want to believe that her sister had anything to do with bringing the entity here or waking the nightwraith. Then again, how well did anyone know another?

They had been raised in the same house, but they had spent decades apart, each taking a different path. It was only over the past three years that she and Savita had been brought back together. And in that time, both had changed a great deal.

"What if it's Savita?" Esha looked at Kendrick. "What if I'm wrong, and my sister turned on us?"

Kendrick drew in a breath and slowly released it. "I think it's one thing to want to keep you from spending time with me. It's quite another to send something like the nightwraith. I could see it if she sent it after me." Kendrick turned his head to Dain. "Are you sure Esha is the target?"

"That's what I heard. And my sources are reliable," the Dark replied.

That confused Esha. "Why me? I've done nothing other than be a Ranger."

"Until I arrived." Kendrick's lips flattened. "Perhaps they think they can no' harm me, so the next best thing is to go after you in case an alliance develops."

An alliance of a kind *had* happened. Esha couldn't understand why they wouldn't want an ally. "I'm not the only elf who met you," she pointed out.

"You're the only one who wanted to track with him," Dain stated.

Esha cut her gaze to him. "You're with us. Why didn't the nightwraith get sent after you?"

"I don't share my business with others," Dain replied flatly.

She threw up her hands in frustration and let them slap against her thighs. "I want to find what's killing elves and stop it. What's so wrong with that?"

"It's no' the *why*, lass. It's the *who*." Kendrick sighed. "It comes back to me. If I hadna crossed onto Shecrish, I doubt this would be happening."

Dain shrugged indifferently. "We can't change what's happened. Things have been set in motion. I'm not going to stop looking for the being, but I think it's going to be more difficult since we'll have to look over our shoulders for the nightwraith now, too."

"*Our?*" Esha asked. "You're including yourself now?"

He swung his yellow gaze to her. "It will smell me here."

"But Esha has a point. It isna after you," Kendrick said.

Dain paused before he nodded. "True. What are you thinking?"

Kendrick studied him for a moment before his gaze landed on her. "We have two choices. We trust each other or we doona. If we work together, there's a chance we can sort this out. Otherwise, we go our separate ways right now."

Dain was the first to speak. "I've been trying to track the entity thing on my own. I've gotten nowhere, and I want retribution. I *need* it."

"All right," Kendrick said.

Esha swallowed as she struggled to decide.

"Have I ever wronged you?" Dain asked her in a flat voice.

She shook her head.

"Has any Dark Elf?"

Reluctantly, Esha shook her head again.

"Then you're going off what others have told you." Dain sneered. "If I did the same, I would never trust any elf other than a Dark. You think you've heard horrible things about my people? I've heard far worse about every other class of elf. Not everything we're told is true. It's why I make my own decisions."

Well, when he put it that way, Esha felt like a fool for putting up such a fuss about him. "You're right. I'm sorry. I've had little dealings with Dark Elves. Based on what I've heard, I tend to keep my distance."

"I've stated my intentions," Kendrick said. "I'm willing to trust both of you."

Dain rolled his eyes. "You're a Dragon King. If you get tired of us, you can return to your land."

"But I willna."

No, Esha knew Kendrick wouldn't. If she had learned anything about him, it was his true and loyal heart. She met his gaze and smiled. There was so much she wanted to say about their night together, but she didn't know where to begin. And what was there to say? It was the best night of her life, and she hated that it would be the only one like it. But she had known that going in.

What she hadn't counted on was the pain she felt knowing she wouldn't share another night with Kendrick. It was crushing, like the weight of a mountain resting on her chest. What would she do if he wanted another night with her? Would she be strong enough to refuse him? Esha honestly didn't know.

She could tell herself that no one would know if she were with him again, but *she* would. She would carry that with her, letting it corrupt her each time she stood with her fellow Rangers, all of them having taken the same vow. The Rangers were all Esha had ever wanted.

Weren't they?

She looked at Kendrick, and for a moment, she allowed herself to imagine what it might be like if they could have as many nights as they wanted. The problem was, there were too many variables and things she didn't know. He was from Idrias, and he would return to the dragons soon. She didn't belong there any more than he belonged on Shecrish. So where did that leave them?

The same place they had begun—apart.

"Where do we go now? What do we do?" Dain asked. "Keep hunting the entity? Do we look for Savita? Maybe find who roused the nightwraith? Or, I suppose, we could face the beast."

Kendrick shrugged as he looked at her. "I didna place a time limit on this mission. Savita did. If I caused any of this, then I want to be the one to help right it. I'll go wherever you want."

So, the decision rested with her. Wonderful. She was used to turning to Savita and having her consult the runes. Now, Esha was unsure what to do. What seemed the logical move? No one had been able to track the invisible entity. As for her sister, Esha wanted to get more information before she rushed around looking for Savita. The biggest concern right now was the nightwraith. That seemed the best course of action. Then again, Dain had said it couldn't be stopped. She smiled as she looked at Kendrick. But they had a Dragon King.

Kendrick's lips curved. "The nightwraith?"

"Yes."

"Well, the blending of our eccentric group is going to be short-lived," Dain mumbled. "You know we're all going to die, right?"

Esha chuckled. "Not all of us."

"I can no' know that for certain. I've never faced this creature before," Kendrick added.

Dain rolled his eyes. "Which means I'll be the only one to die."

Kendrick clapped him on the shoulder. "Oh, I wouldna worry, my friend."

"I feel *so* comforted," Dain muttered sarcastically.

Esha laughed despite the circumstances. They were a strange trio, but if they had any chance of survival, it was because a Dragon King had joined them.

"Are you up for taking us back underground?" Kendrick asked Dain.

Esha's stomach twisted painfully, but she kept her thoughts to herself. She had forgotten they would have to return the way they'd come.

"I should be," Dain said. "I'll need a bit to recover before we face the nightwraith, though."

Kendrick shrugged. "There is another way."

"What's that?" Esha asked a little too hastily. She inwardly winced, hoping neither of them noticed that she was ready to do anything but go underground again.

His green eyes met hers. "I can fly us."

"Count me in," Dain said, his eyes as bright as his smile.

Esha hesitated. If Kendrick did that, she wouldn't have to face her greatest fear. However, it would also mean that elves would see him. Word of his arrival might have spread, but no one had *seen* a dragon in generations. How would her people react when they saw him in the sky?

"Everyone knows he's here," Dain said as if reading her mind. "What does it matter?"

She gave him a flat look. "You know why."

Kendrick turned her to face him. "I know it might frighten some elves, but think of it this way. I'll be able to find the nightwraith easily, and it'll keep Dain from draining his magic. We all need to be ready to battle the beast. I'd like to think I can take it down easily, but we can no' know that."

"What if we can't kill it?" she asked.

Kendrick looked away for a moment. "We'll think of something."

"Like what?" She wasn't going to face a nightwraith without a plan and alternative options, even with a Dragon King by her side.

Kendrick turned to Dain. "Is there any way we can turn it off our trail?"

"It can't be reasoned with, if that's what you're asking," Dain replied.

"Have you tried?"

Dain barked a laugh. "No."

Esha watched the exchange with interest.

Kendrick said, "Can Wood Elves no' talk to animals?"

"You want to ask one of them to talk to a nightwraith?" Dain asked in a choked voice.

Kendrick shrugged. "What's the harm in it? Maybe they can persuade it to return to wherever it came from."

"He has a point," Esha said.

Dain blinked a couple of times before saying, "I suppose. Do you know any Wood Elves?"

"We're in a forest," Esha pointed out.

Dain closed his eyes, his face tight as if fighting for patience. When he opened them, he asked, "Do you know one we can *trust*?"

"All we can do is ask. Maybe one of the Wood Elves close by will help," Kendrick said.

Esha raised her voice as she turned in a slow circle and said, "Would one of you be willing to join us in trying to stop a nightwraith from continuing its rampage?"

The silence that greeted her was depressing.

"It was worth a shot," Kendrick told her.

Esha turned back to the guys. "I'd still like an alternative."

"We have to slay an unkillable animal." Dain's lips twisted.

Kendrick blew out a breath. "Then we fight until it's dead. Or we are."

Esha grimaced. She contemplated getting her Rangers, but she knew it wouldn't be fair to ask them to fight the beast on her behalf. "If those are our options, those are our options."

"What are we waiting for then?" Dain asked.

"I can no' shift here," Kendrick said. "I'd take out too many trees, and I'd rather no'."

Esha motioned for them to follow her. "There's a clearing ahead."

As they walked, she kept hoping that one of the Wood Elves would answer her request, but none did. She knew they were there. They hid well in the trees, but they always kept watch over their forests. No doubt they knew why the nightwraith was coming, and they blamed her.

When they reached the clearing, Kendrick nodded. "This will do."

"You sure you want to do this?" she asked.

"It's either I fly us, or we go back underground."

Esha shivered at the thought.

"Exactly," Kendrick said with a smile. "It'll be fine. I promise."

She looked at Dain, who couldn't hide his excitement at the anticipation of flying. Neither of them knew if Kendrick soaring over their land would go over well with their people. Only time would give them that answer.

"You might want to step back," she told Dain as she moved away.

Dain followed her suggestion. When they were far enough away, Kendrick shifted. Even having seen it before, he still awed her.

"By the night," Dain exclaimed in wonder.

She grinned and looked into Kendrick's sapphire dragon eyes. "I know exactly what you mean."

What they hadn't asked was how they would get on Kendrick. Would he carry them in his hands? Paws? What were they? She eyed his talons. They looked like they could easily tear something apart. Perhaps they shouldn't get too close to those claws.

Kendrick lowered to his belly, which gave her the answer she needed. Esha was the first to approach. She reached his front leg. His head swung toward her, and he nodded. She jerked her hand back in surprise when she touched his scales and found them warm and hard beneath her palm. They seemed incredibly thick, as well. She took all of that in as she gingerly climbed up his leg and shoulder before settling at the base of his neck. When she looked around for Dain, she found the elf slowly walking around Kendrick.

"Are you coming?" she called.

Dain appeared not to hear her as he continued the loop and stopped in front of Kendrick. The Dark said nothing as he stared into Kendrick's eyes. She leaned to the side to see Dain. She wondered what he was thinking. After a few minutes, the elf climbed up the same way she had, though he paused to inspect Kendrick's scales in much more detail than she had.

Finally, Dain settled behind her. That's when they both realized they had nothing to hold on to. Her heart dropped to her stomach when Kendrick climbed to his feet. Even that small movement made her realize how precarious their positions were. She tried to clutch Kendrick's scales, but she couldn't get a good grip.

"He won't drop us," Dain said.

Esha tried to reply, but she couldn't find her voice. Kendrick spread his wings, and she grabbed his scales, hoping she could hold on. A shriek fell from her lips when Kendrick leapt into the air. His wings flapped, the *whoosh* loud as he climbed higher and higher.

"This is amazing," Dain said with a laugh.

Esha's heart thumped wildly in her chest until Kendrick's body leveled out. When she no longer felt as if she would fall to her death at any second, she looked down to see the land below them, nothing but a blur. She smiled and let the rush of air whipping over her ground her in the moment. This definitely beat going into the dark, dank underground.

Chapter Nineteen

Kendrick's gaze scanned far ahead as he flew. As soon as he shifted, he notified Con about what was happening. It took some doing to keep him and the other Kings from crossing onto Shecrish, but in the end, they realized it might not be ideal to cause even more of a stir.

Kendrick hadn't been sure how he would feel about having someone on his back, but he found he didn't mind it. It wasn't as uncomfortable or awkward as he'd thought it might be. Yet his range of motion wasn't as unrestricted as it normally was. He was all too aware of the two elves clinging to him. The slightest wrong move could cause them to slip off.

He grinned when he heard Dain chuckling. The Dark Elf was clearly enjoying himself. Esha was coming around. She no longer had a death grip on him. His thoughts halted when he spotted a small cloud of smoke rising from the forest in the distance. He rose a little higher in the sky to get a better look and saw that large sections of trees had been felled. It didn't take long for him to find what was responsible.

The animal was twice the size of a blue whale. The nightwraith was a pale gray color and moved wickedly fast. The devastation it left in its wake was unbelievable. The trees hadn't just been downed, the thing had shredded them. Kendrick hoped that if any elves or animals were nearby that they had gotten clear.

Kendrick flew faster. Neither Esha nor Dain had noticed the beast yet. Kendrick went through his options. If he were alone, he'd dive at the beast and battle it from the air, but he couldn't do that with the two elves on his back. They might be able to hang on for a bit, but his attention would be divided, which wouldn't do any of them any good.

The best thing to do would be to land now and get Esha and Dain somewhere safe. They would most likely argue, but he didn't intend to listen. Kendrick hadn't fought a nightwraith, but he had a better chance of surviving than his companions. He wouldn't tell them that because they would argue that they should fight together. Esha would claim the creature was after her, but Kendrick wasn't so sure. It seemed more likely that he was the target. Who had sent it was another matter. But he'd get to the bottom of that soon enough. First, he had to handle the rampaging creature.

Kendrick looked for a place to land. He found an area far enough away from the nightwraith that it would keep Esha and Dain safe until he finished with it. As he descended rapidly, Esha's fingers gripped his scales.

Behind her, Dain said, "There it is. What are you doing, Kendrick? Go toward it."

Since he couldn't speak to them telepathically, there was no way to tell them his plan. Which was good because he didn't have time to argue his point.

"He's not taking us to it," Esha told Dain.

Kendrick tilted slightly to one side, then the other. They both held on tightly. He hoped that proved his point, but when Dain began arguing, Kendrick knew the elf hadn't gotten the message.

"We'll join the fight one way or another," Esha told him.

Kendrick growled, letting the sound rumble through him.

Esha leaned low and said, "You know I'm right. Take us. We do this together."

Kendrick continued his trajectory to land, when he happened to glance toward the nightwraith. The animal locked eyes with Kendrick and halted in its tracks. It was unlike any animal Kendrick had ever seen. It had a large head with a massive mouth and enormous fangs. Mammoth-sized tusks protruded from either side of its head and extended past the creature's shoulders, curving upward into sharp points.

The nightwraith's upper body was humanoid. It had long arms with three digits on each hand tipped in claws. It looked like it had plating over its thick skin along its arms and up to its shoulders, but as Kendrick flew closer, he realized it was the shards Dain had mentioned. The lower half of the beast looked like a snake, and the nightwraith used it as efficiently as a dragon did its tail.

It was headed right for them.

"Kendrick!" Esha shouted.

He dipped his right wing slightly to move away, but the creature matched him immediately. There was no way he could get Esha and Dain to safety on the ground before he and the animal collided. Kendrick could turn around, but that would put more elves in the nightwraith's way. By the way it homed in on him, Kendrick knew the beast had been searching for one of them.

Kendrick quickly scanned the area and saw nothing but trees below him. The nightwraith had laid waste to much of it, and Kendrick wished they were in a more open space, but there was no time for that. His real concern now was his friends on his back.

In the middle of formulating a plan of attack, Kendrick caught sight of something. He spotted the shard from the nightwraith just before it tore through his wing. Kendrick jerked his wing up, which caused his body to tilt. He felt Esha slip from his back, and his heart leapt into his throat.

"More shards are coming!" Dain shouted in warning.

Kendrick hoped the elf was holding on because all he cared about right now was getting hold of Esha. Kendrick caught sight of Esha falling and spun around. Dain tried to hold on, but he fell, too. The Dark Elf managed to grab hold of Kendrick's wing. Kendrick dove for Esha and snatched her out of the air with his hand. He glanced down at her to see her holding on to him tightly before she lifted her head and met his gaze.

Dain pulled himself up and climbed back into position just as a dozen more shards came at them. Kendrick tucked his wings and dove, but he wasn't quick enough. One of the shards struck him where his wing met his body. He let out a roar of rage as pain burned through him. Thankfully, Dain pulled the spike out, easing some of Kendrick's pain.

They were on the defensive, and that wasn't how Kendrick wanted this battle to go. He could use dragon fire, but it would decimate the forest. He would leave that as a last resort. He had some other tricks up his sleeve. But first, he had to get the elves to safety.

"Fly low," Dain shouted. "Really low. I'll jump off."

It was a decent plan, but it wasn't without consequence. Yet it gave Kendrick what he needed.

"Drop me with him," Esha said.

A growl rumbled through Kendrick when another volley of shards came at them. He turned himself to keep any from finding their mark in Dain, though two other slivers sliced through his wings, and a few bounced off his scales.

Kendrick swung back toward the nightwraith. He spotted an area the creature had cleared in its furious search for them and dove toward it. Kendrick tucked his wings and held his hand against him to protect Esha. Dain leaned forward so his upper body was flush against Kendrick's scales.

As Kendrick neared the ground, Dain pushed up with his hands and got his feet beneath him. Kendrick hoped the elf realized when it was time, but he shouldn't have worried. Dain waited until the last possible second and then jumped clear, tucking his body and somersaulting in the air twice before landing on his feet. At the same time, Kendrick lowered his arm and opened his hand. Esha jumped safely to the ground, pulling her sword from its scabbard as she did.

Kendrick wanted to see if they were all right, but he kept his gaze on the beast before him. He could've sworn the animal smiled as he approached. Kendrick kept his wings tucked against him as the nightwraith released more shards. They bounced off Kendrick. He flew over the animal, just out of reach. The creature screamed in fury and turned to track him. Which meant it never saw Kendrick's tail coming at it.

The barbed end embedded in the creature's neck. Kendrick spread his wings and flew upward, intending to drag the nightwraith with him. But the animal was more clever than he realized. As he climbed, the nightwraith managed to get its mouth around his tail. Its shards might not be able to penetrate Kendrick's scales, but it was intent on sinking its fangs into him.

With a flick of his tail, Kendrick released the nightwraith and watched it plummet. Kendrick dipped a wing and swung around as the animal crashed into the ground. He hoped it was enough to kill the creature. He stared for a heartbeat before sweeping the nearby area for Esha and Dain. To his relief, he saw both elves running toward the nightwraith. They halted when they caught sight of the thing.

Kendrick was about to land when he saw the beast move. To his shock, the nightwraith pulled itself up and looked around for its target. Kendrick roared a warning at Esha and Dain as he flew over the animal and raked his talons down its back.

The nightwraith screamed in pain and rage. Kendrick quickly zoomed upward as shards came at him again. More cut through his wings, leaving behind sizzles of pain. He finally halted and hovered far above the animal. Kendrick looked down to find the nightwraith trying desperately to jump as if it could reach him.

Kendrick readied for his next attack when he saw Esha and Dain coming at the nightwraith from different directions. Everything Dain had said about the beast rushed through Kendrick's head, and all he could think about was Esha being killed.

Nay!

No one heard his bellow. Kendrick tucked his wings and dove again. This time, he was sure the creature smiled. Kendrick didn't care as long as its attention was on him and not his friends. The nightwraith lowered itself as if it were about to spring. It had learned from Kendrick's previous attack. The animal was smart *and* clever, a deadly combination for sure. No wonder Dain was terrified of it.

That didn't stop the Dark Elf from attacking, though.

Right as Kendrick flew over the nightwraith, Dain appeared behind it and plunged his sword into the animal's back. It screamed and turned to strike Dain. Esha ran toward the nightwraith, her sword glowing gold. She jumped and sliced the beast's neck and then rolled away right as Kendrick raked his claws over the beast again.

He sighed when Dain used the shadows to get both him and Esha clear. Then Kendrick circled back around for another strike.

Chapter Twenty

Esha couldn't believe the nightwraith was still alive. But Dain had warned them that it was hard to kill. She just hadn't expected it to be *this* hard.

The animal was bloodied, and she imagined it had broken bones, but it didn't seem to notice. It'd set its single-minded focus on Kendrick. Which made her wonder if he was the target. If it had been her, the nightwraith would've noticed her by now. Instead, it seemed locked on Kendrick.

Shadows appeared on the opposite side of the clearing, and Esha watched as Dain stepped out of them. He grinned at her before his attention swung to the battle. Dain would make an excellent Ranger. When this was over, she'd talk to him about joining. He probably wouldn't, but there was always a need for those with his skills.

Esha locked on to Kendrick. He was magnificent. The way he moved with such ease was something to behold. Then there was how he used his wings, tail, and talons to attack. She wondered why he hadn't breathed fire, but maybe that was because she and Dain were so close.

She glanced at the nightwraith, who watched Kendrick and hunched down as he neared. Kendrick dove toward the beast. Halfway down, Kendrick suddenly disappeared. Esha glanced at Dain, who shared a shocked look with her. Even the nightwraith seemed confused as it searched for Kendrick.

Esha stilled as the animal locked on her. It growled angrily and began stalking toward her. She swung her sword around her, calling to the sun to enhance her weapon again. It looked like the beast was after her.

"Run!" Dain shouted.

But that wouldn't do any good. The nightwraith had its sights set on her, and it wasn't going to alter its course. Esha didn't look away from it as she wondered where Kendrick had gone. It never even entered her mind that he had left them. He wouldn't do that. She lifted her sword and felt the magic sizzling from the sun's warmth, the power moving down the blade to the hilt and through her hand. She prepared to engage the beast when a gust of wind ruffled her hair, sending it into her eyes.

A heartbeat later, the nightwraith let out a bellow. Esha saw long grooves open on the beast's back as blood gushed. She spotted Kendrick's sienna scales as he flew away. The beast chased after Kendrick, who coasted low to the ground.

Esha started to follow, but Dain grabbed her arm. "What are you doing?" she demanded.

"He's leading it away."

She jerked her head back to Kendrick. He swung around in a tight circle and moved his wings in front of him for a heartbeat. He hovered in place as the nightwraith raced toward him. Kendrick didn't move as the creature jumped into the air, shards raining from its arms and fangs extended.

Esha saw Kendrick's chest expand as he drew in a deep breath. There was a pause before he opened his mouth, and a torrent of fire shot out. It consumed the nightwraith instantly. It shrieked as it fell to the ground, flopping as it tried to get away. But it fell silent within seconds.

"Fuck me," Dain murmured.

Esha swallowed, nodding numbly. She knew that dragons were powerful, but this was so much more than she expected.

Kendrick didn't stay there. He flew so high that she lost track of him. Even when she shielded her eyes from the sun, she couldn't find him. The fire devoured the beast, bones and all, faster than she had ever seen a blaze burn. Then again, it *was* a Dragon King's fire.

She had even more questions for Kendrick now that she had seen him fight. She couldn't wait until he returned. Her stomach clenched. *Would* he return? She looked up at the sky again, but there was still no sign of him.

"He'll be back," Dain said matter-of-factly.

She glanced at the Dark. "You can't know that."

"You can't be so blind that you don't see the way he looks at you."

Esha lowered her gaze to the ground. She couldn't hear this. It would make things more difficult. "It doesn't matter."

"Ah. The Ranger code."

She heard the scorn in his words. Esha faced him. "Do you have a problem with our way of life?"

"You're telling me that you don't care for Kendrick?"

"I asked you a question."

"And I asked you one in return," he retorted, the look in his yellow eyes hard.

Esha drew in a deep breath. "I gave a vow."

"Which means you won't see if anything could come of you two."

"It's what I have to do."

Dain snorted in derision. "That's shite."

"We have our reasons."

"Right," he said sarcastically. "You need to be focused."

She held his gaze and lifted her chin.

"Do you think your Rangers are the only group of warriors? The Dark have something similar, and we don't keep those who have skills from having loved ones or a family. And you know what, Ranger? We do just as well as you."

"It's our way. I made my decision when I took that vow."

Dain shook his head dismissively. "I suppose that means you and Kendrick will just be friends. I'm sure, after all of this, he'll continue to come to Shecrish. I've no doubt the Dark council will want to meet with him. I'm sure others will, as well. It might take some time before things can become truly friendly, but in the meantime, he'll be here. Meeting other elves. Most likely, the most beautiful will be paraded in front of him."

She knew Dain was trying to anger her. Unfortunately, it was working. The thought of Kendrick spending time with other women brought a storm of jealousy that threatened to choke her. But what could she do? She had no future with Kendrick. She had been over this with herself already. The only partner she would ever have was the Rangers. Not an individual—the group.

"That prospect doesn't appeal, I see," Dain said. He eyed her and briefly lifted his brows. "You can change that."

"You assume I have more power than I do."

"I don't think you claim enough."

She hesitated, hating how his words held a ring of truth. "It doesn't matter. Kendrick isn't here. He might not come back."

"If you believe that, then you *are* blind, Ranger." He shook his head and looked away for a moment. "You're a warrior. Ever think you could still be that *and* be with Kendrick?"

"I know that's not possible."

"Then maybe you don't deserve him."

Dain walked to the dying embers of what was left of the nightwraith. Was Dain right? About any of it? She couldn't say for sure. She knew she didn't belong with the dragons, and he didn't belong here.

Esha couldn't help but look skyward again. There was still no sign of Kendrick. Her heart felt heavy. She'd thought she would have time to say farewell. Though, if she were honest, she could admit that she hadn't even thought of that. She'd been too caught up in the night before.

The way his arms had felt around her. How his hands had wrung so much pleasure from her. How he'd kissed her as if he might die without her. How their bodies had fit together so perfectly. She didn't want to say goodbye. Ever. Even if she did walk away from the Rangers, there was no guarantee that she had a future with Kendrick.

But she wanted to find out.

He desired to become allies with her people. Those in power might balk at the idea at first, but they would eventually come around. There were too many reasons for them not to. Dain was right. Kendrick would be back. Often. They could sneak in some time together, but the more likely scenario was that his days would be booked solid.

She knew how beautiful some of those in the city were. They pampered themselves all day to achieve such looks. Would one of them turn his head? Would one of them catch his eye? Would they learn the taste of his kiss or the softness of his lips? Would they discover how astonishingly easily he could wring a climax from them?

Would he hold them tenderly afterward?

Esha sheathed her sword as a dull ache bloomed in her chest. She knew what she wanted. And she knew what she had vowed. She could leave the Rangers. No one was held to the order if they wished to give up their position. But it was all she had ever known. What would she do? Join the Dark army? That certainly wasn't likely. She also wouldn't sit around and wait for Kendrick to visit. She would lose her mind.

Would she be allowed to cross onto Idrias? What would she do there? It wasn't as if there were other elves across the border. Would the dragons even accept her? They didn't need elf warriors. She rubbed her head, wishing there was an easy answer.

Esha heard the flap of wings before she saw Kendrick. The joy that erupted within her made her weak in the knees. He flew slowly over her, just missing the tops of the trees. The ground shook slightly as he landed and tucked his wings against him. He shifted and smiled at her.

She ran to him, throwing her arms around him. He laughed as he wrapped her in his arms. They stayed like that for a moment, just savoring each other. She was well aware of how badly things could have gone for them.

Kendrick pulled back to look at her. Then he kissed her softly, letting his desire gradually fill her. She clung to him, wondering how she would ever let him go. When the kiss ended, they were both breathing hard.

Esha touched his face. "I didn't think you were coming back."

"I wanted to make sure there were no other creatures out there."

His green eyes were so bright. She could stare into them all day. "You killed a nightwraith."

"It left behind a lot of damage," he said with a frown.

"The Wood Elves will see it repaired," Dain said as he walked to them. "Glad to see you in one piece."

Kendrick released Esha as he faced the Dark. He grinned and said, "I wasna sure the beast would die."

"Too bad we can't bottle your fire," Dain said with a chuckle.

Kendrick looked at Esha. "Shall we find your sister now?"

"Yes." How could she have forgotten about Savita? "I'd like to go to Flamefall and talk to those there. They may have information."

"Want me to fly you?" Kendrick offered.

She wanted nothing more but knew she couldn't let him see their base. "Not this time. Before I go, tell me why it looked as if you disappeared."

"Every dragon has a special ability," he explained. "I can camouflage myself."

Dain snorted loudly. "Now that is an ability I'd like to have."

"You can travel with shadows," Esha stated.

Dain's smile widened. "Jealous?"

"Yes. Surprised?" she countered with a grin.

Dain nodded once. "I am."

They shared a smile. Esha hadn't thought she would ever call a Dark a friend, but she could see Dain becoming one. She felt Kendrick's gaze on her and turned to him. "Will you be here when I get back?"

"Of course."

"Even if it's past the three days Savita gave us?"

Kendrick's smile was slow as it curved his lips. "Even then."

Dain groaned. "You two are killing me. Esha, want me to take you to the lake?"

"Please," she said.

She moved to Dain, but she never took her eyes off Kendrick, even when the shadows wrapped around her. When they dispersed, she was at the lake. She looked at the water and thought of Kendrick walking from it. So much had happened since they had set out.

"Think about what I said."

She turned to Dain. "Why do you care?"

"We still haven't found our common enemy. How are we to do that if Kendrick leaves?"

"Hunting that thing doesn't require us to be romantically linked."

Dain sighed loudly. "I guess that means another Ranger will hunt with us."

"I don't think so."

He merely grunted in response as the shadows took him.

Esha turned and started the trek to camp. She went directly to Savita's tent, but it was empty. Then she began asking around about her. It didn't take long for her to determine that her sister had left right after she had the day before.

Esha went to her tent for a change of clothes. A folded piece of paper sat on her bed. She opened it to find a note from Savita.

E –

Trust me.

S.

Esha changed and folded the note to tuck into her shirt before exiting her tent and then the camp.

Chapter Twenty-one

When he was finally alone, Kendrick breathed a sigh of relief. He turned his head to look at what remained of the nightwraith. Then he made his way to it. The fire still blazed, but he'd made sure to contain it so it didn't spread. As he stood near the crumbling remains, Kendrick thought about the viciousness of the creature. The way it'd moved, its cunning. The shards might not have pierced his scales, but the ones that'd penetrated his wings had left behind some discomfort.

It wasn't as bad as what a Dark Fae's magic felt like, but it was close. No wonder elves were terrified of the beast. Its tracking ability alone was enough to give even him pause. Would it have ever stopped looking for its target? He wished he knew—that and which one of them it had been after.

He knew the instant he was no longer alone. Kendrick didn't look up from the ashes as he banked the fire with a thought, but he sensed he was being watched from the trees. Wood Elves, no doubt. He hoped they understood that he was a friend.

Kendrick looked into the forest before him. He waited until an elf showed himself. High in the tree on a thick limb, a body moved away from the trunk. Kendrick bowed his head in greeting. The elf then jumped from the tree and landed softly as if leaping from a mere few inches instead of dozens of feet.

The male was tall and slender. He strode calmly to Kendrick, halting on the other side of the ashes. The Wood Elf's skin was a copper color. He had the top half of his dark red hair tied behind his head, and the rest of it fell just past his shoulders. Green eyes regarded Kendrick solemnly. The tunic and pants the elf wore were simple in design, but the material was anything but. He held a bow in his left hand, the quiver of arrows resting on his back.

"I'm sorry about the destruction," Kendrick said.

The elf's gaze briefly moved to the side to take in the downed and splintered trees. "It's been ages since a nightwraith ventured from underground."

"We heard it was after one of us."

The elf quirked a red brow. "You don't know which of you it sought?"

"Unfortunately, we don't. You wouldn't happen to have that answer, would you?" When the elf said nothing, Kendrick replied, "I didna think so." He paused, studying the elf. "I came to your land to hunt a mutual foe. The one that no one can see. I heard it's attacked several elves."

Still, the Wood Elf said nothing. So, he tried again. "My name is Kendrick. I came hoping our people could be allies. I've been tracking with a Ranger and a Dark Elf."

"We saw."

"Is there any way I can help with any of this?" Kendrick asked and swept his hand around to indicate where they had battled.

The elf glanced at the ashes. "It seems you already have."

"I'm no' your enemy."

"If we thought you were, we would've attacked instead of approaching."

Well, there was that, at least. Kendrick glanced at the woods around him and saw more elves. They were in various locations in the trees. "I've heard the Wood Elves are some of the best fighters."

"*The* best." Then the elf grinned. "I'm Tarron."

"Pleased to make your acquaintance. Do you lead the Wood Elves?"

Tarron shrugged a shoulder. "Something like that. You are all anyone can talk about."

"I imagine. Where I'm from, there are no elves."

"Really?" Tarron's brows shot up on his forehead. "I take it Esha has told you about us."

"She has."

"I gather the Dark has, too."

The hardness in his words warned Kendrick to tread carefully. "I'm learning from everyone. Dain has helped us."

"A Dark Elf might lend aid, but they always want something in return."

"Aye. He asked to join us in tracking our mutual foe."

Tarron's eyes narrowed. "That's it?"

"That's it."

"What will you do if you discover the nightwraith was after you?"

Kendrick shrugged, his lips twisting. "I suppose I'll discover who sent it so I can talk to them and hopefully change their mind about wanting to harm me."

"Many believe your arrival will bring more dragons."

Which was the exact reason Kendrick had told Con not to come. "That isna our intent. I'm sure you'll hear a lot, so let me clear up a few items. The dragons are content on our land. However, something *is* attacking us. I'm a Dragon King. It means I can shift at will. No' all dragons have that ability, and, aye, there are more like me. I come in peace, but I *will* defend myself, as you've seen for yourself."

"You give me a lot to think about."

"Which I hope you will. I also hope you'll tell others that I can be a friend, and that I *want* to be an ally."

Tarron nodded slowly. "I feel no lie in you, Kendrick. I've witnessed your power. I think if you wanted to take our lands, you could do so easily."

"Something is harming others that wasna here before." Kendrick hesitated for a moment and then continued. "I'm no' from this world. The dragons here are descendants of ones who came from my realm of Earth."

Tarron's brows snapped together briefly. "Did someone take the dragons like they take us?"

"Nay."

"Do you know who brings us here?"

Kendrick shook his head. "Regrettably, nay."

"If you discover the truth, would you share it with us?"

"I will."

Tarron walked around the pile of ashes and placed his right hand on his heart as he bowed his head. "You will be welcome in any forest, Dragon King."

"Thank you."

"Your Dark friend is waiting for you. He's been listening for some time."

Shadows moved from the forest, and Dain emerged. "You knew I was there?"

Tarron snorted. "Of course. Shadows don't hide you in our domain."

Kendrick motioned for Dain to come closer. "Tarron, this is Dain. Dain, Tarron."

"I know who he is," Dain stated tightly.

Tarron eyed him. "Good. Then you know where you stand."

Dain's expression hardened. Kendrick put a hand on his chest and met his gaze. After a moment, Dain relaxed a fraction.

Kendrick blew out a breath. "Tarron, my offer stands. This mess was caused because the beast was after one of us."

"Most likely sent by this Dark."

Dain took a step toward him. "Watch your tongue, Wood Elf."

In a split second, every elf Kendrick could see—and probably those he couldn't—had an arrow nocked and aimed at Dain. Kendrick moved between the two elves. He looked from one to the other. "There's bad blood between your people, but that doesna mean it has to be between the two of you. Tarron, Dain is the one who warned us about the nightwraith."

"No Dark would ever send one of those creatures after anyone," Dain stated angrily. "Few understand the violence a nightwraith can exact like the Dark Elves do. We live among them. We do *everything* to keep away from them. Only those who don't understand the ferocity of that animal would stir it and send it from its home."

Kendrick swiveled his head to Tarron. "You said that you didna feel a lie in me earlier. Can you do the same with Dain?"

"Yes," Tarron bit out.

Kendrick waited for him to expound on that. When he didn't, Kendrick prodded him. "And?"

"I sense no lie."

Dain glared at Tarron. "Because I'm not lying."

Tarron nodded once. The elves lowered their bows.

Kendrick breathed a sigh of relief and took a step back. He was beginning to understand why the Dark didn't venture from their underground homes if they were constantly met with such open hostility from others. Then again, there were always two sides to every story. He wasn't there to mend centuries of hate and anger.

Tarron turned his attention to Kendrick. "Good luck in your endeavor. We're also hunting this concealed creature. If I hear anything, I'll let you know."

"Thank you." Kendrick wondered how Tarron would do that, and he was looking forward to finding out.

"Tread carefully, Dark," Tarron said. "We'll be watching you."

Dain smirked. "How could you not when I look this good?"

Tarron rolled his eyes and walked past them to the forest. In a blink, the elves were gone, or at least hidden from view.

Kendrick faced Dain. "Did you have to provoke him?"

"He irks me," Dain said with a shrug as if that were explanation enough.

"What about Esha?"

"We got to the lake fine. She was in a hurry to get answers—not that I blame her."

"Aye. Me, either."

"Are we waiting for her?"

Kendrick thought about that for a moment. "How long would it take for her to reach us?"

"A while." Dain suddenly grinned. "Are you offering a ride?"

Kendrick chuckled. "We need to get to her." His smile died as he thought of Savita's disappearance. "What do you know about Esha's sister?"

"She was all anyone could talk about for some time. The Reader who left the city to join her sister's Ranger group."

"Esha said that hasna happened before."

"It hasn't. I'm sure you can imagine the stir it caused."

"I can," Kendrick said with a nod. "How many Readers are there?"

Dain scratched his jaw. "I don't know the exact number, but I think it's somewhere around fifty."

"What did you hear about Savita?" Kendrick asked.

"That she is a talented Reader—more so than others. Each Reader is born with the ability, but a few are more attuned to the runes than others."

"And that was Savita?"

Dain shrugged. "So it's been said. Belanore wasn't happy to lose her."

"But no one questions the Readers."

"Exactly," Dain said with a twist of his lips.

Kendrick couldn't help thinking that something was going on with Savita. "Has any Reader ever lied?"

"If one has, we'd never know." Dain chuckled. "The life of a Reader is based on truth. They report what the runes tell them. No one questions them, so how would they get caught if they did lie?"

Kendrick crossed his arms over his chest. "Readers are in positions of power. Where would Savita hold a better station? With the Rangers or in the city?"

"The city, without a doubt."

"That's what I thought, too."

Dain jerked his chin to him. "What are you thinking?"

"I'm thinking something's going on. Savita disappearing just as a nightwraith attacks us makes things pretty clear."

"You think she did it?"

Kendrick wrinkled his nose. "I think she didna like my arrival. I think she didna like Esha wanting to hunt with me."

"You'd think she would make sure dozens of Rangers were with you two."

Kendrick frowned. "Aye. I thought the same. But does that mean she sent an animal she knew could kill her sister? I doona think she did."

"Unless she knew you could defeat it."

"What would she gain by doing that?"

"Other than showing everyone your strength? I don't know," Dain said with a shrug.

Kendrick could throw out a hundred guesses, but the elven society was different from any he knew, which put him at a disadvantage.

"Go find Esha," Dain said as he turned on his heel to walk away.

"Where are you going?"

"To talk to my contacts," the elf said over his shoulder.

Kendrick waited until the shadows had claimed Dain before he shifted and jumped into the sky. He took his time flying and getting a better view of the plateau and its many lakes, waterfalls, and the large river that cut through the land. It was a beautiful area, and he had made inroads into becoming allies with the elves.

But he was still no closer to finding the entity than before.

Chapter Twenty-two

Esha reached the lake and heard the unmistakable flap of wings. She looked up and spotted Kendrick as he circled above her. The relief she felt at seeing him made her lightheaded. There was a smile on her lips when he landed. She quickened her steps to reach him.

When she saw his grin when he spotted her, she thought of Dain's words again. Esha wouldn't be able to stand seeing Kendrick with anyone else. For now, however, it was just the two of them, and she was grateful not to be dealing with this alone.

"Savita asked me to trust her," she said once she reached him.

Kendrick frowned and parted his lips. Before he could speak, she handed him the note. He opened it and read it before refolding it and handing it back to her. "Do you know where she went?"

"It could be anywhere."

"You said she was upset before we left. Based on that note, she knew you would look for her. It's her way of telling you not to."

Esha briefly closed her eyes. "I'm not sure I can do that. What if she's in danger?"

"I suspect your sister is more than capable of handling herself."

"She's not a Ranger."

Kendrick's green eyes were solemn. "Nay, lass. She's a Reader, and she has a tremendous amount of influence. I doona think you need to worry about her needing to defend herself with a weapon."

Esha shook her head in agitation, knowing he was right. "The only place I can't go is the Reader Temple. There isn't a need for fighters there because they don't use weapons when they spar."

"It's political. Does she go often?"

"From time to time. But she's never left camp like this before."

Kendrick took her hand in his and gave her a reassuring smile. "If you can't go to the temple, then you have no choice but to do as she requested and trust her."

"Why didn't she talk to me?"

Kendrick rubbed his thumb across the back of her hand. "Does she normally?"

"It's been a long time since either of us has confided in the other. Sometimes, it's hard to believe she's the same girl I used to follow around the house, trying to emulate. Anything could have upset her. I don't know what was in her head."

Kendrick tugged her against him. "That's no' true. You knew the runes kept warning her about danger."

"If she kept at it, which I know she would have in order to get to the bottom of it, then she might have found something." Esha leaned back to look into his green eyes. "She might irritate me, but she's the only family I have left. You might not understand that because we're not related by blood but—"

Kendrick put a finger to her lips to silence her. "My family is long gone. The other Kings are my brethren, and their mates are my sisters. Blood doesna always make a family."

She smiled up at him. "No, it doesn't."

Someone cleared their throat behind Kendrick. Esha looked to find Dain. The Dark's lips were pinched, and unease filled his gaze.

"What did you find?" Kendrick asked as he turned to face Dain.

Dain's yellow eyes briefly met Esha's. "Nothing good."

"Tell us," she urged.

When the Dark was silent for too long, Kendrick said, "Dain."

Dain sighed loudly. "Savita is with the Conclave."

"They called her?" Esha said, fear gripping her. It was never good when the Conclave took an interest in someone.

Dain shook his head. "She sought *them*."

"Why?" Kendrick asked.

Dain swallowed nervously. "Apparently, she wished to speak about Esha."

"Why would she do that?" Esha couldn't imagine a scenario where her sister would do such a thing.

Kendrick's voice was low and dangerous when he said, "Savita claimed the runes told her something, didn't she?"

"Yes," Dain replied.

Esha looked between them. "So, what did the runes tell her?"

"That was all my contact knew." Dain put up his hands placatingly. "I swear."

Esha's heart raced, and her ears started ringing loudly. Savita had really gone to the Conclave. But…why? Sure, they'd fought, but nothing that would send Savita to do something so drastic. At least, not without talking to Esha first. What could the runes have possibly told her? Whatever it was, it was important enough for the Reader to take such a step.

And that couldn't be good for any of them.

Esha continued searching her mind for possibilities. Then she looked at Kendrick. The runes could've told Savita about their night together, but Esha hadn't broken her vow yet. She inwardly cringed at the last word of her thought. The mere fact that it'd come up told her she wouldn't have the power to resist Kendrick. There was something between them. She had felt it before giving him her body. And their night together had only strengthened the connection.

"Esha?"

The sound of Kendrick's lilting brogue made her want to seek comfort in his arms and the passion that would allow her to forget—at least for a time. But she couldn't. If she turned to him now, it would be harder to stop herself the next time.

"Esha," Kendrick called again.

She lifted her gaze to his, then followed his finger as he pointed behind her. Esha caught sight of her sister standing just inside the trees. Savita's face gave nothing away, but somehow, that only worried Esha more.

Esha glanced around for Dain. "Where is he?"

"Gone," Kendrick replied.

"I have to go to her," Esha said.

"I'll be here."

Esha nodded without looking at him. She walked to her sister, noting that Savita had her gaze downcast. When she reached her sibling, Savita turned and strode into the woods. Esha glanced back to see Kendrick standing alone.

"I take it you know where I went," Savita said.

Esha had to try twice to swallow. "The Conclave. Why?"

"There were things I had to tell them."

Savita was usually cagey when she had something important she needed to keep to herself, but she was acting particularly guarded now. Esha knew it was about her, and she feared that her sister knew that she struggled to stay away from Kendrick. "I've had a really long day. Just tell me whatever you need to say because I can't take the anticipation."

"You never could." Savita glanced at Esha. "I know about the nightwraith. And you riding atop a dragon. I also know Kendrick killed the nightwraith."

"Did you hear someone sent it after me?" Was it her imagination, or did Savita's steps falter?

Savita's shoulders lifted as she took in a deep breath. "Yes."

"Did you send it?"

Savita halted and spun to look at her with shock. "You can't seriously think that."

"You went to the Conclave about *me*. What else am I supposed to think?"

"I didn't send the nightwraith, and I'm hurt you'd think I would do such a thing to *anyone*, much less you."

Esha stared at her sister, wanting to believe her, but there was no denying the doubt in her heart. "Why did you go to the Conclave?"

"I told you. There were things I needed to convey to them."

"About me?"

Savita sighed loudly. "Not everything I said was about you."

"Am I being removed as a Ranger?"

"What? Of course, not."

The shock on Savita's face looked genuine, but Esha wasn't sure about anything anymore. "Then why go to the Conclave about me?"

"I told them it was time they ranked you higher. After all, you were the one who realized the implications of having a Dragon King as an ally. You also saw the wisdom of hunting the entity with Kendrick when no one in your squad nor anyone else in our camp would have."

Esha was so surprised she could only stare at her sister and blink.

"You doubt my motives." There was sadness in Savita's words. "I admit, I don't like Kendrick, but not for the reasons you think. From the moment you brought me to meet him, I saw how you looked at him. As if he were some mystical being who had all the answers."

Esha was taken aback. "He's a shifter. A *dragon* shifter. One who is much more powerful than any elf."

"Impressive, yes."

Esha narrowed her eyes. "What aren't you telling me, sister?"

"I've known about his arrival for some time."

Esha stumbled back a couple of steps and braced herself against a tree with her hand. She shook her head as she struggled to figure out what her sister was about. Because if there was one thing she knew about Savita, it was that her sister always thought several steps ahead of anyone else.

"The runes told me a few years ago," Savita continued. "They told me how important he would be—to you."

"Does he mean me harm?"

"Never. I made sure of that."

"Then why try to keep us apart?"

Savita gave her a dry look. "Do you really need to ask that? Tell me, sister, how was last night?"

Esha looked away and fought to rein in her riot of emotions. "I'm granted one night."

"You are, yes. But it was more than that. And don't attempt to lie. The runes told me the truth, even if you won't acknowledge it."

Esha closed her eyes and leaned her cheek against the tree. The bark was rough against her skin.

"You want to know why I went to the Conclave? Then I'll tell you," Savita said as she walked closer and lowered her voice to barely a whisper. "I went because Kendrick's arrival fractures everything we know. Everything we are. There were already deep cracks, but there is no fixing them now. There hasn't been for some time. There are those who want him as an ally, and those who are so opposed to the idea that they'll do whatever is necessary to stop it—and anyone who dares to side with him."

Esha's eyes snapped open as she looked at her sister, anguish and indignation roiling within her. "You know who sent the nightwraith."

"Not yet. But I know it *was* sent after you."

She didn't want to believe it. How could any of her people do that to her? Esha couldn't even comprehend it. "As a warning?"

"They thought it would kill you *and* Kendrick."

Esha snorted. "Then they know very little about dragons or Dragon Kings."

"Be that as it may, things are in motion now that cannot be stopped."

"You're a Reader. They must believe you."

Savita smiled sadly. "Ah, sweet sister, you know it isn't so simple. The Conclave has their own Reader, for one."

"Then what do we do?"

"I put the word out about you being brave enough to hunt with

Kendrick against the thing killing elves. Many are singing your praises right now, as well as Kendrick's for stopping the nightwraith. But that will only buy you a little time. If he remains in Shecrish, then this fracture will continue to grow. It's divided our people, and it will end with those angry about Kendrick's arrival crossing onto Idrias."

Esha gaped in astonishment. "They'll be annihilated. If everyone knew the story of the dragons, then they would understand why it's imperative we keep off their land."

"Nothing anyone says will change what is happening."

"And if Kendrick leaves?"

"There is a chance we can repair what has happened. Though it's a slim one."

"The fear and distrust are already seeded among those who believe the worst about Kendrick and his motives. That won't ever change, will it?"

Savita took her sister's hands in hers. "I don't know."

"You do."

It was a full minute before Savita spoke, a single tear falling down her cheek. "No. Those elves won't change."

"There's a reason the dragons have a border around their land they don't want crossed. Everyone knows that."

"That was before a Dragon King came to Shecrish. They're furious that the dragons believe they can come onto our land without retribution. Not to mention that Kendrick showed his might in killing a creature that no elf can."

"The nightwraith was after me and destroying everything. What choice did he have?"

Savita nodded sadly. "You know how fear works, sister. It removes reason from the equation."

"We had a chance to find the invisible foe and kill it. For us and for everyone on Zora. Now, I have to tell Kendrick to leave because elves fear his power."

"Simply put, yes. Then we begin working to change the minds of those who fear the most and have the loudest voices. We convince everyone to leave the dragons alone. The other option isn't one I even want to consider."

Esha didn't need to ask her sister what the runes had told her to know that it would mean the end of the elves if an army crossed the border. The last thing she wanted was to send Kendrick away, but she didn't have another choice. Her wants meant nothing compared to tens of thousands of lives.

She looked through the trees toward the lake and Kendrick. "I should tell him tonight."

"Would you like me to do it?"

"It needs to come from me." Esha pulled her hands from her sister's and started back to Kendrick.

Chapter Twenty-three

Kendrick was thinking of all the ways he could spend his last day with Esha. He wouldn't push her to spend another night in his arms, but that didn't keep him from hoping she would. There were all kinds of ways he could seduce her, but he had too much respect for her and her vow to the Rangers to do that.

One more day. That's all he had, and he would make the most of it. If they caught their foe, perhaps it would earn him some more time amongst the elves. There was so much more for him to learn.

He was grasping for reasons to remain so he could get more time with Esha. He still hadn't figured out how to tell her that she was his mate. They hadn't known each other long, and she might not believe him. He probably wouldn't if he were in her shoes. Yet he knew the truth of it with as much certainty as he had known so long ago that the magic had chosen him to be the King of Siennas.

Kendrick needed more time with her. He didn't want Esha to leave the Rangers and wished she didn't have to, but they couldn't be together if she were still part of the organization. It hurt his heart that she would have to give up something she loved so deeply for them to be together.

Time. He needed time. It was something he'd always had plenty of before. Yet now it seemed to slip through his fingers no matter how hard he tried to slow it. There had to be another way to prolong his visit. He had to show her how good they were together. He needed to let her discover that she loved him, too. Allow him to prove his love and devotion.

Because the alternative meant that he had fallen for someone who didn't love him.

And that thought made him ill. A dragon couldn't survive without their mate. Once a dragon found a mate, it was all that mattered until they were together. No matter how long it took, no matter what Kendrick had to do, he *would* win Esha's heart.

Movement in the trees drew his attention and pulled him from his thoughts. He spotted Esha and relaxed. A part of him had worried that Savita would keep her talking for hours, cutting into the precious time he had left with her. It was a good sign that the sisters finished early. Wasn't it?

Kendrick met Esha halfway. Her smile was tight, forced even. His heart skipped a beat. Something was wrong. *Very* wrong. He searched his mind for possible reasons and found dozens. Despite the unease churning ominously through him, he knew how important hunting the entity was to Esha. If nothing else, he would have that.

So little fucking time. He inwardly scowled at all the moments he had hurried time along. It had never occurred to him that he might run out. Eons and eons of years of life, and he had only a handful of hours now with the one person who mattered the most to him. The irony didn't go unnoticed.

He tried to think of something to make her smile and ease the tension, but his mind was blank. "I take it the talk with your sister didna go well."

"You could say that." Esha glanced at the ground and shook her head.

"Did she turn on you?"

"Actually, she petitioned the Conclave to give me a higher rank, citing I was the only one intelligent enough to see the benefits of befriending you."

The words said one thing, but her voice said quite another. It felt like something was tightening around Kendrick's chest. "That should be something to celebrate. Why are you no'?"

"Your arrival has…divided our people."

Kendrick's blood ran like ice in his veins. He blinked in disbelief. "I want a peaceful alliance. I told you that from the beginning."

"I know. There are those who believe that and wish to become allies."

"But others doona." It was a kick in the stomach that he should've expected.

She nodded solemnly. Esha's golden-amber gaze held regret and sorrow. He knew what was coming, and he wanted to stop her. Because if she didn't say the words, then everything could stay the same. Yet all he could do was stand there in excruciating agony as she spoke.

"The best thing would be for you to leave. Now," Esha said. "Those who want you as a friend are trying to dissuade the others from attacking."

Kendrick fisted his hands as he briefly closed his eyes. There was already a war brewing on the dragons' eastern border. They didn't need to worry about someone else coming after them. All because he had thought he could cross onto someone else's land and be welcomed. It didn't matter how many times he said he wanted peace, there would always be those who thought he lied.

"If any elves cross the border, we will attack," he cautioned her.

Esha swallowed. "That's another reason. We're not allowed to go onto your land without reprisal. The Conclave feels the same should apply to any dragon or King who comes onto ours."

As much as it irked Kendrick, it was only fair. The dragons had wanted to be left alone, and Eurwen and Brandr had guaranteed that. Then the Kings found the dragons and remained on Zora. Instead of continuing that peace, their actions had pushed other beings into fear and attack mode.

"You understand, don't you?"

He nodded slowly, trying to find his voice in the emotions clogging his throat. "I'm sorry. For all of this. You're right. I need to leave immediately. If you think it would help, I can talk to the Conclave myself."

"It won't. Not now, at least. I'm not sure it ever will. You must understand, we've not seen a dragon in generations. Some have been pushing to send Rangers to Idrias to see if any remained."

"Doona do that. Make sure you tell them that no one can cross. Please," he pressed.

"I will."

Kendrick took a step toward her. This wasn't how he'd wanted their time to end. He'd assumed he had at least one more day. How he wished he could halt time. This could be the last time he saw Esha, the last time he touched her, held her. Kissed her. He had one chance to do and say everything he'd thought he had a day to do. There wasn't time for pretty words. Just the simple truth.

Would it be enough? He prayed it would. But what if it wasn't? What if she refused him? It was too much for Kendrick to even contemplate, even though there was a real possibility it might happen.

He looked into her eyes and struggled to find the right words, ones that would convey the depth of his feelings. "Before I go, there is something I need to tell you. Do you remember when I said dragons know their mates?"

"Yes."

"It wasna a lie. I need you to believe that."

"I do," she said softly.

Kendrick took her hands in his. He glanced down at them, remembering how it'd felt to hold her in his arms. It seemed like a lifetime ago. When he imagined never touching her again, the agony took his breath away. He pushed that aside and focused on the words. "I found my mate in you. Before you argue," he said when she parted her lips to speak, "I know what I feel. You may think it's too soon, but I would argue that we've been through a lot in a short time. We fought side by side, opened up about ourselves and our people, and shared our bodies. You know there's something between us. You felt it, too, or you wouldna have come to me."

"I'm not denying it. To do so would be to belittle the best night of my life." She smiled, though it held a note of sadness. "But that's all it can be. One night."

"There could be more. So much more." He was reaching for anything, even as he felt himself tumbling into an abyss of darkness and anguish.

"If we had met under different circumstances, and if we were different people, I would say you're right. But we aren't. You are a dragon. I'm an elf."

He was losing her. He could feel it. "We need more time."

"Our time is over. You must leave now to prevent a war, and I have a duty to help others calm those who want to cross into Idrias."

"I love you, Esha. Come with me," he said in a last-ditch effort to keep them together.

Esha looked at the ground and shook her head as she pressed her lips together. "You're asking me to leave my land, give up my position, and forfeit everything I know and love to go to a place I'm not welcome."

"You'd be with me."

She took a deep breath and looked into his eyes. "My place is here. Your place is with your people. Please, Kendrick. Go. Now."

He could do nothing but stand there as she pulled her hands out of his and walked away. "Esha!" he called. But she didn't slow.

Kendrick watched her walk away, each step feeling like the turn of a dull knife being shoved into his heart. He was a dragon of great power, yet he had never felt so helpless, so…powerless.

"If you change your mind, you know where to find me!" he shouted after her. Then, in a whisper, he added, "Look back at me. Please, look back at me."

She entered the forest without a backward glance.

Kendrick looked around in a daze, hardly believing that his mate had just left him. He contemplated taking Esha and convincing her of his love, but he knew how ridiculous that sounded. He shifted and thought about flying to the cities to talk to anyone who would listen, but he would likely only make things worse. Esha was right. The only thing he could do was leave, even though it killed him to do it.

He spread his wings and took to the air. As he rose, he spotted the Ranger camp. He wondered if Esha was looking up through the trees at him now. But the thought only brought him more pain. Kendrick turned his gaze to the east and flew fast to the border. He didn't pay attention to the landscape below him. He didn't look for the invisible entity who had attacked both dragons and elves. All because he was drowning in anguish and heartache.

When he flew through the barrier that separated the dragon lands from the elves', he wasn't surprised to find Con on patrol. Con's gold scales flashed in the sunlight. As soon as he saw Kendrick, he headed toward him. The last thing Kendrick wanted to do was talk, but the sooner he got it over with, the sooner he could be alone. Kendrick landed and shifted.

When Con arrived, he did the same. The King of Dragon Kings took one look at him and frowned. "What happened?"

Kendrick ran a hand down his face. "Too much. No' enough."

For the next thirty minutes, he relayed everything that had happened since his last check-in, including the nightwraith attack.

"Bloody hell," Con muttered. He glanced away as he shook his head. Then his black gaze settled on Kendrick. "Leaving was your only option. We doona need a war with another group."

"That's why I'm here."

"I know you're hurting, brother. I remember the pain of no' having my mate well."

"Aye, but you and Rhi are together now. I lost my chance with my mate," Kendrick argued.

Con stared at him silently for a long moment. "Let things settle down with the elves. We'll try again."

Kendrick was suffering now, and Con wanted him to wait? Most likely years. How would he survive? "They're right. We shouldna be allowed to cross without the same retaliation we threaten them with."

"I could argue that Erith created this realm for dragons and no' anyone else."

"Be that as it may, other beings are here. We might be the strongest, or we may no', but that doesna mean we can pick and choose what we want to apply to us."

Constantine wiped all emotion from his face. "Do you want the same thing that happened on Earth to happen here? Do you want the dragons fighting for their lives again?"

"You know I doona," Kendrick snapped.

"Should we allow the children with magic to continue being slaughtered? Do we stand idly by and do nothing as other individuals with magic run for their lives so they are no' killed or enslaved?"

"Nay, we shouldna. But in helping those people, we're going onto their land. We shouldna be surprised when they fight back."

Con sighed. "Nay, we shouldna."

Kendrick was tired of talking about this. "Please tell me you've heard from Merrill."

"Nothing. Brandr has checked in with Eurwen as he continues his trek around the realm. He's no' seen or heard anything about Merrill." He paused. "You should come to Cairnkeep and relay all this information to Eurwen."

"I've been away from my post for too long. Thank you for covering for me."

Con studied him. "Everything you learned about the elves needs to be shared with others."

"I know. I just need...a few days."

"Of course."

Kendrick waited for Con to leave, but the King of Dragon Kings remained. "I'll be fine. I just want to be alone."

"You know we're here for you."

"I do."

With that, Con shifted and flew away. Kendrick breathed a sigh of relief as he returned to dragon form and took to the skies. He made a pass along the border, doing his patrol. He tried not to look across or think about Esha, but he was as successful with that as attempting to stop his heart from beating. After two passes, he gave up and went to sit on the cliff.

Kendrick returned to his human form and let his feet dangle over the side of the rock face as heat waves rippled across the land. He felt something beside him and turned his head to see the Pink.

Ceri unfurled a small wing and touched his arm with it, her emerald eyes meeting his.

"Thank you for going to Cairnkeep," he said.

He heard a snort in his head. Then she said, "*Someone had to watch your back.*"

"I knew I'd win you over." He tried for a teasing tone, but it fell flat.

The Pink tucked her wing against her body and settled beside him.

Kendrick's gaze drifted toward Esha's location as he sank deeper into depression.

Chapter Twenty-four

Six weeks later...

Esha entered her tent and slumped into a chair as she dropped her head to her hands. She tried not to think about how long it had been since Kendrick had left. She tried not to think about him at all—but failed miserably. Meditating or awake, he was always on her mind.

She winced as she sat up. The aches and pains from the thieves her squad had fended off did nothing to take her mind off Kendrick. Not a day had gone by without some scuffle or incident since he'd returned to Idrias. Word of him had spread far and wide across Shecrish. She couldn't enter Rannora or Belanore without a bard singing of Kendrick's power, or someone debating the bias of elves not being able to visit the dragons as Kendrick had so easily crossed onto their land.

Just as Savita had warned, the elves were divided. Those who wanted the dragons as allies didn't hesitate to tell her as much, but it was the ones on the opposite side who were the loudest and most vocal—and they seemed to be winning.

For every elf who spoke about the dragons with fear, Esha tried to get them to see the benefits of having the dragons as friends. Somehow, the conversations always turned to Kendrick not being punished for coming to Shecrish, when they were promised death if they crossed the border into Idrias. It was the argument being waged the loudest among those who wanted to ensure that no dragon ever returned.

Esha was exhausted mentally, physically, and emotionally. She hadn't given herself time to mourn Kendrick. Mostly because she knew if she did, she would have to admit how much he meant to her. That would lead to nothing but heartache.

"I found my mate in you."

Esha squeezed her eyes closed as she heard Kendrick's voice in her head.

"I love you, Esha. Come with me."

"Stop," she demanded in a hoarse whisper as she pressed the heels of her hands against her eyes. Only when she was sure she wouldn't hear his voice again did Esha lower her arms. She opened her eyes and caught sight of the hem of Savita's white gown. Esha sat up and looked at her sister. "I didn't hear you come in."

Savita said nothing as she walked farther into the tent. She stopped beside the table and ran her finger along the scabbard that held Esha's sword. "You look tired."

"A few days of rest would be nice."

"I wish I could give them to you."

Esha sat back in the chair and raised a brow at her sister. She was too tired for this. "What is it?"

"Do I need a reason to see my sister?"

"Of late, yes." It was true. They hadn't seen much of each other lately. Partly because Esha had been breaking up raids but also because Savita had been spending an exorbitant amount of time traveling back and forth to visit the Conclave.

Savita sighed. "Some of us are actively working to calm things down. It's taking longer than expected."

"Is that why you're with the Conclave so much?"

Savita hesitated before saying, "They ask about you."

"Of course, they do," Esha replied sarcastically. "Kendrick is gone. What more do they want from me?"

"They want you to tell them everything Kendrick shared about the dragons."

Esha got to her feet, anger making her seethe. "No."

"I've had to disclose a few things you told me."

"You promised you wouldn't tell anyone. You agreed that they would somehow use it against the dragons."

Savita lifted a hand to quiet her. "I had to give them something or they were going to bring you in. I didn't share the story of what originally brought the dragons here. No one needs to know about the goddess. That *would* be used against the dragons."

Esha crossed her arms over her chest. She knew Savita was protecting her, but she was still angry about everything. "What did you tell them?"

"How powerful they are, especially the Kings. I told the nightwraith story again and how Kendrick defeated it. I'm not the only one speaking about it. A Dark Elf, Dain, has been very vocal about Kendrick's usefulness. The way Dain talks, he was at the battle."

Esha said nothing. She hadn't seen Dain since Kendrick left. She didn't even know how to contact him. If she even had time for such things.

"Tarron of the Wood Elves is also speaking highly of Kendrick," Savita continued. "Tarron is widely respected, so his word carries a lot of weight. His people who witnessed the battle are telling everyone they come across about what Kendrick did. I'm trying to help, Esha."

Esha dropped her arms to her sides. "I know. It just feels as if it's a losing battle. All Kendrick did was help. He protected me. Not once did he attack anyone."

"It isn't about that."

"Yes, yes. The border. He came to Shecrish," she said with a roll of her eyes. "The horror. The dragons could wipe all of us out with barely a thought, and yet some elves want to attack them. It's ludicrous."

Savita's shoulders drooped. For the first time, Esha noticed how fatigued her sister looked. Savita leaned her hands against the table to brace herself.

"Have the runes shown you or any Reader a way to end this?" Esha asked with a concerned frown as she eyed her sister.

Savita was silent for a long time. "There has been unrest among the elves for a while. Much longer than anyone knows. But it was at least kept somewhat contained. Those in power who have pushed to see if the dragons were gone from Idrias are now turning that to a demand for anyone who comes onto our land to be detained, possibly with lethal results."

"You didn't answer my question."

Savita lifted her head and met Esha's gaze. "Yes. The runes showed me a way to end all this."

The news shocked Esha. The excitement and hope that rushed through her left her knees weak. "When? Never mind. That doesn't matter. What is it? Have you told anyone?"

"Eventually, a few elves will cross the border. The dragons will attack. And elves will die. It will enrage those who have supported the dragons."

Esha blinked at the bleak future her sister put before her. "I thought you said you knew of a way to end this."

"I do."

"That isn't a way. That will begin an all-out war, and we don't stand a chance against the dragons."

Savita nodded slowly. "I know."

Esha shook her head, refusing to believe this. "No. There has to be another way. Surely, the idea of our annihilation should put a stop to all this nonsense."

"I'm not the only Reader who was shown this outcome."

Esha paced the tent. For a split second, she'd felt hope that this chaos could be stopped, but the answer was worse than she could comprehend. "You told me to send Kendrick away. You told me that would stop things."

"I said it should."

"He's gone. No dragons will be coming to Shecrish for the foreseeable future. Probably not ever." She couldn't think about the knot in her chest that the idea of never seeing Kendrick again caused.

"I know it's hard to believe, but that's because you haven't been made aware of the things going on politically."

Esha halted and spun to glare at Savita. "No one gives a shite about that. This is about our lives! Our very existence." She covered her face with her hands and tried to calm the riot of emotions. If she could get word to Kendrick and warn him what Savita had seen, then the dragons might be able to come up with a way to stop the war. But…that would mean going to Kendrick. There was no way he could come back across the barrier to her.

Her heart raced at the thought of seeing him. It would only be for a moment, but it would bolster her. And, hopefully, she'd save her people.

"You used to do that when you were younger."

Savita's words pulled Esha out of her thoughts. She lifted her head, frowning. "What?"

"Pace and cover your face when you were thinking over a difficult problem." Savita grinned as she straightened and walked to Esha. "I always thought your mind was moving so quickly that your body had to do something to try to keep up."

Esha grinned. "Something like that."

"Rest, sister. We've a long road ahead of us."

"You should take your own advice."

Savita shot her a sad smile. "I'll try." She turned to go, then paused and faced Esha. "I know you think I lied to come here with you. I didn't.

The runes guided me."

"Did they tell you why?"

Savita's eyes danced with delight. "Of course."

"You aren't going to tell me?"

"What would be the fun in that?"

Esha chuckled as she shook her head at her sister. "You've been a pain in the ass, but I'm glad you're here."

"Me, too." Savita held her gaze for a moment longer before turning to leave.

Esha returned to her chair and sank into it once more. She couldn't stop thinking about what Savita had told her. There couldn't be a war. It wasn't fair to the dragons or the elves. The only way to stop it was to get word to Kendrick. Esha thought about trying to find Dain, but she didn't have a clue where to begin. Try as she might to find another way, it ultimately fell to her to get to Kendrick.

With the decision made, she began planning how to do it. She went about her evening as normal: bathed, had dinner, spoke to her squad. She almost stopped by Savita's tent to tell her sister what she was doing, but it would likely be better if no one knew. Besides, if everything went according to plan, she would be back by dawn. But that meant she had to get moving.

Esha wove through the dense jungle of trees. She nodded to the Rangers on watch. It wasn't odd for her to be out at night, so no one paid much attention to her. Once at the lake, she moved quickly to make her way to the edge of the plateau, and then down.

Sweat covered her by the time she jogged toward the barrier. Her eyes scanned the darkness for any signs of movement, be it animal or elf. Esha hoped that Kendrick was there. He had told her she would know where to find him. That had been weeks ago, though. Would he give up so easily? She hoped not.

Was she prepared to look into his green eyes again? To hear that sexy voice? Could she withstand the desire that flared anytime she was near him? For every day they had been apart, a part of her soul had withered away. She hadn't wanted to believe him when he said that she was his mate, but she knew it was true. She missed him so much that she could barely carry on and get through each day without him, and the closer she got to the border, the more that ache grew until it nearly consumed her.

Her heart thudded loudly in her chest. She had turned away from him once. How would she do it a second time? She couldn't think about that now. She needed to focus on finding him and relaying the information.

The border loomed before her. A quarter moon hung in the clear sky, but no dark shapes of dragons flew near it. Esha slowed to a walk. She'd half-expected Kendrick to see her so they could talk without either of them crossing the boundary. That way, neither side would be incited.

She quietly drew her sword when she heard a whisper of sound. When she turned toward it, she saw a Ranger with his weapon raised, running at her before shadows abruptly overtook him. She stared in shock as the Ranger fell to the ground, and the shadows moved away to reveal Dain.

"Did you kill him?" she demanded of the Dark.

His lips flattened in annoyance. "It's nice to see you, too. And, no, I didn't kill him. Though I should have, given what he intended to do to you."

"What are you doing here?"

"Helping you."

Esha turned her head from one side to the other, searching for other Rangers. "What are you talking about?"

"Savita sent me."

"What?" she asked in a shocked whisper.

Dain walked to her. "Rangers are guarding the border. Savita knew you would need help."

"That's not possible. I'd know if Rangers were guarding the border."

"They kept it from you."

She narrowed her eyes on Dain. "Why?"

"Because they feared you would do exactly what you're about to do."

Esha only became more confused. "Who?"

Dain sighed as if it put him out to be the one to fill her in. "I told Savita we should tell you, but she said it had to be your decision to go to Kendrick."

"Tell me everything. Now," Esha demanded as she pointed the edge of her sword at Dain's throat. The fury that consumed her was so thick she wasn't sure she could control it.

Or if she wanted to.

"All you had to do was ask." He shoved aside her blade with a finger. "I'd planned to tell you."

Esha lowered her weapon. The muscles in her jaw ached as she clenched her teeth together. "Then talk."

"The runes told Savita about those on the Conclave who saw you as a threat. They're the ones who released the nightwraith. Fools," Dain ground out with hostility. "They will pay for that."

"Why are they afraid of me? I'm just a Ranger."

Dain snorted loudly. "The Conclave Reader told them the stones had shown you and Kendrick together in a romantic relationship. It would give the elven people a strong ally, but those opposing that have other plans."

"So, I had to die?" It was too much to grasp.

"They didn't think the problem through, or they would've realized that if Kendrick somehow survived, he wouldn't let you die."

"They had no way of knowing that a Dragon King could kill a nightwraith."

Delight shone on Dain's scarred face. "No, they didn't. I wish I could've seen their faces."

"If I am supposed to be with Kendrick, why didn't Savita tell me? Why did she let me sit here for weeks without him?"

The Dark shrugged. "As she said, you had to decide on your own. And she wanted to see how others reacted."

"Is she in danger?"

"We're all in danger," Dain said with a shrug. "Don't worry about your sister. She's craftier than I gave her credit for. She found me, and that isn't an easy thing to do. Even for a Reader."

Esha glanced behind her to the plateau. She thought of Flamefall, of her Rangers, and of Savita. "What happens now?"

"You warn Kendrick, which will hopefully stop the war. We're going to get to the bottom of who is pulling the strings here. I have some ideas, but it's going to take more digging."

"Will you look after Savita?"

Dain issued a bark of laughter. "As if she would allow that. Your sister will be fine. But, yes, I will keep an eye on her."

"Thank you."

The Dark placed his right hand over his heart and bowed his head. "Tell Kendrick hello for me. I hope to see both of you again."

"We will."

"Go, Sun Elf. I'll make sure no one stops you."

Esha had the sudden urge to hug him. She nodded and sheathed her sword. Dain grinned before calling the shadows to him and disappearing. Then she started running toward Idrias and Kendrick.

No one tried to stop her again. She didn't look behind her to see if anyone would. She kept her gaze locked on where Shecrish ended and the land of the dragons began. When Esha crossed through the barrier, the feel of the magic sweeping around her was like a soft hum. Then she stood on dragon land, her heart hammering again.

Suddenly, a dark shape appeared from a nearby mountain. Wide wings spread as the dragon flew straight at her. She knew without seeing the color of the scales that it was Kendrick. Elation and a tiny bead of panic rushed through Esha. The excitement was too much to contain. Esha didn't hide her smile as she watched the beautiful dragon approach.

Chapter Twenty-five

Ceri had told him about the elves near the barrier. Kendrick had locked eyes on them and immediately recognized Esha. He hadn't been able to move for fear that she would vanish before he could get to her. When he glanced over to see who she spoke with and noticed Dain, he didn't dare let himself hope that Esha had come to him.

Then she crossed the border.

Kendrick had taken to the skies in an instant. He wanted to get to her quickly, but he was also afraid of scaring her. But as he approached, he saw her smile. Just to be safe, Kendrick turned at the border and flew along it to see if anyone had followed her. He spotted a few elves who appeared to be guarding the barrier, but that was all. When he flew back to Esha, he saw an elf on the ground where she and Dain had been.

He landed before her and shifted. They stared at each other, neither moving. Six long weeks had passed since he had last laid eyes on her. It felt like six lifetimes. He raked his gaze over her, but he didn't see any injuries.

"Am I…welcome?" Esha asked hesitantly.

Kendrick grinned, his heart ready to burst from his chest. "Oh, aye, lass. Absolutely."

That's all it took for her to rush to him. Kendrick met her halfway and wrapped his arms around her. Their lips met in a passionate, fervent kiss filled with desperation and yearning. He touched her face, her hair, marveling that she was in his arms again. He had to know that this wasn't a dream, that she was real.

He looked down at her. "I didna think you'd come."

She hugged him tightly.

He felt a shiver go through her. "What is it?"

"There's so much I need to tell you."

Kendrick leaned back and met her gaze. "About the elves?"

"They intend to come and start a war. We need to stop it."

"If they cross, there isna much I can do."

Her golden eyes implored him. "Please. We have to try."

"Then you need to tell us what's going on. We'll have questions."

She hesitated but then nodded. "I understand. My only stipulation is that it happens here. Just in case they try something soon."

Kendrick glanced across the border, where he saw the elves watching them. He took her hand to lead her toward the mountain. "We've been vigilant since I returned. Give me a second to notify the others."

Kendrick opened his mental link and sent out a call to Con and Eurwen. Both answered immediately and said they were on their way. Flying wouldn't have taken too long, but Rhi teleported them instantly.

"An elf," Rhi said and smiled at Esha. "What a pleasure it is to meet you. Kendrick has told us all about you, but I have so many more questions."

Kendrick chuckled. "We'll get to that. First, introductions. Esha, this is Rhi. She's a Light Fae and mated to Con, King of Dragon Kings." Kendrick motioned to Con, who stood to Rhi's right. He bowed his head of wavy blond hair to Esha. "To his right is their daughter, Eurwen. She rules Zora with her twin brother, Brandr."

"I'll fill him in on everything," Eurwen said. She turned to Esha. "I'm sad to say we didn't know about the elves. We kept to ourselves, and now I'm seeing that was the wrong thing to do."

Kendrick didn't know if Esha realized the powerful beings she stood before, but she didn't seem cowed by them. She had her guard up, but that was to be expected.

"It's nice to meet each of you," Esha replied. She glanced at him. "Kendrick told me some stories."

Rhi twisted her lips. "Yikes. I'm not sure I want to know what those were."

"You know exactly which they were," Con said with a chuckle.

Esha tilted her head when Rhi spoke. "Your accent is different."

"Kendrick, Eurwen, and Con have Scottish brogues, while I have an Irish accent," Rhi explained.

"Places on Earth," Kendrick told her.

"So," Eurwen said as she glanced toward the barrier, "not to cast a shadow on this meeting and new acquaintance, but why are we here?"

Esha licked her lips and looked at Kendrick. "How much did you tell them about my culture?"

"Everything you told me," he assured her.

Esha took a deep breath and released it. "My sister, Savita, was right. The elves are divided. The loudest are the ones opposed to making an alliance with the dragons. I just learned that there has been dissension among the elves for some time. Savita said it had been contained as best it could be, but Kendrick's arrival changed everything."

"Because I came onto your land without any ramifications," he said.

Esha met his gaze and nodded. "Those elves want revenge, and they plan to cross the border."

"That would mean war," Eurwen replied coolly.

Kendrick grunted. "I think that's the point."

"I don't understand," Rhi said. "Surely, the elves realize they'll be killed."

Esha shrugged. "I think they're hoping to take down a dragon or two. They don't understand the magnitude of what they're doing."

"Nay, they doona," Con bit out.

Esha swallowed nervously. "If my people come, and you attack, it will be the end of the elves. Those fighting for an alliance will swiftly turn against the dragons."

"Bloody hell," Eurwen muttered.

Kendrick nodded in agreement. "It's the dissenters' way of turning all elves to their side."

"But it will likely kill all of them. Why would they do that, simply to prove themselves right?" Eurwen asked.

Esha shrugged helplessly. "I can't answer that. I'm merely repeating what Savita told me. I had no idea that she had sought out Dain after Kendrick left. The two of them have been working together."

"I never would've guessed that," Kendrick said. "What are they doing?"

"Trying to learn the identities of those on the Conclave who sent the nightwraith after me."

Kendrick stilled as her words sank in. "What?"

Esha winced. "I imagine I had that same look when Savita told me. It seems the runes told some of the Readers that I'm the answer. That if I'm with you, there will be no war."

"So they sent that creature to kill you?" Rhi asked in shock.

Kendrick grunted. "One impossible for an elf to kill."

"Luckily for Esha, you're no' an elf," Con said.

Esha chuckled softly. "You didn't face it. Trust me, I know exactly how lucky I am."

"So," Rhi said, tapping the toe of her black stiletto boot, "you're telling me that some arseholes are so worried about you befriending a Dragon King that they sent a beast to kill you? I don't think I like these elves."

Esha grinned in response. "Savita and Dain are going to continue their work. They're intent on discovering the names and stopping those elves." She cut her gaze to Kendrick. "They're worried I'll become much more than a friend to Kendrick."

"Ah," Con said with a nod.

Kendrick couldn't allow himself to even consider that Esha was here to stay for good, to be his mate. It was all he wanted, and he didn't think he would survive it if she left again. He turned to Eurwen. "I did go onto their land without permission. Whether we think it right or no', we shouldna get a pass to go wherever we want if we doona allow the same on our land."

"Brandr and I have been discussing it since you returned." Eurwen nodded at her parents. "It's also a topic that comes up often with my parents, as well as Vaughn. You know why no one is allowed on our land."

Kendrick jerked his chin to Esha. "And yet, there are exceptions."

"This is difficult," Rhi said. "Obviously, it's something that still needs to be discussed. For now, though, I think a decision needs to be made regarding what happens if elves cross."

Eurwen was silent for a moment. "I don't want a war."

"No one does," Rhi replied.

Con shoved a lock of hair from his eyes. "We doona have to attack them."

"A show of force," Kendrick said with a smile.

Con grinned, nodding. "Exactly. Sometimes, that's all it takes."

"Brandr will be sad he missed this," Eurwen said and nodded. "We'll try it. Let's hope it stops the elves."

Rhi took Con's hand. "We should let the others know."

"You two stay here. Kendrick, if you see anything, send word," Eurwen said.

Kendrick bowed his head. "Of course."

"Esha," Con said. "I've a feeling we'll be seeing more of you."

Then the three were gone, leaving Kendrick alone with his mate. He turned to Esha. "Is your sister going to be safe?"

"She's clever and smarter than most. I'd put the odds in her favor, but she's not foolish enough to dismiss the perils of what she's doing."

"Are you going back?" They were the hardest words he had ever uttered.

Her golden-amber eyes held his as she shook her head. "I made my decision."

"Will the elves allow you to return to see Savita?"

Esha glanced at the ground before shaking her head. "We might be able to meet at the border."

"I'm sorry," he said as he pulled her into his arms.

"Savita knew you were coming."

That surprised him. He looked down at her. "The runes?"

"They told her all of it, apparently. She didn't tell me to come to you. I made that decision, but according to Dain, that was exactly what had to happen."

"But she knew you were coming to me?"

Esha's eyes swam with tears. "Yes. I now know that our last conversation was her way of saying farewell."

"It doesna have to be forever. We'll find a way for the two of you to see each other again."

She swiped at a tear. "I knew what I was doing by coming here. It was what I wanted all along, but I didn't think I could do it. I thought it would start the war if I left with you."

"It doesna matter. You're here now," he said and lowered his head to kiss her gently.

"Do you…do you still feel the same?"

Kendrick gazed into her beautiful eyes and smiled. He gently ran his fingers from the points of her ears down her neck. "Do I find you the most beautiful woman I've ever seen? Aye. Do I crave your touch? Do I yearn for you beside me? Do I ache to be inside you? Do I long to see your smile and hear your voice? Do I love you beyond reason or doubt? The answer, lass, is a resounding aye. You're the other half of me, my mate. I feel it here," he said, putting her hand over his heart.

"I may not be a dragon, but I know we're meant to be together. I tried not to think of you so it wouldn't hurt so much, but you were always there. I love you, Kendrick, King of Siennas. I love you so very much."

"Tell me you're staying."

"Just try to get rid of me," she said with a grin.

Kendrick laughed as he lifted her into his arms. He had almost given up hope that he would have his mate, but here she was, in his arms. Whatever came next, they would stand together.

United.

Epilogue

A week later...

For seven days, Esha had been dreading when the elves would come. She had begun to hope that Savita had been wrong, but she should've trusted her sister.

"It's going to be fine," Kendrick said.

She stood on the cliff and kept her gaze on the approaching Rangers—some were even from her old squad. Though there were only about fifty of them, they were the best of their warriors. It had been decided that Kendrick would be the only dragon the elves saw before they crossed the border.

He took her hand in his. Esha looked at him and smiled. The unimaginable joy of being with him the past week had been everything she could have imagined. She'd met more Dragon Kings, including Eurwen's mate, Vaughn. Kendrick had told her that when things were calmer, he would take her to meet Jeyra, Tamlyn, and Nia, all three of which were from Zora. She would even get to visit Dreagan, which was the Kings' home on Earth.

But first, they had to deal with the elves.

"It's time," Kendrick said as he moved away and shifted.

He dove straight down and shot up fast, a roar sounding around her. It gave the elves pause, but they kept coming. When Kendrick swung back around toward her, Esha ran along the cliff's edge and jumped off to land astride him. She leaned low, letting the wind whip over them both, never taking her eyes off the Rangers.

Some of the elves saw her astride Kendrick and halted, but the rest kept coming. One by one, they crossed into Idrias. The minute the last one did, Kendrick let out another roar as he soared over them.

The Rangers released a volley of arrows. They bounced off

Kendrick's scales, with a few coming close to finding their mark in her. With the Rangers focused on them, the elves didn't see the other dragons descending from the thick clouds above.

Con landed before them with such force that the elves fought to stay on their feet. They gawked at the gold dragon. Soon, Eurwen's peach scales and gold wings swooped down to land. Vaughn followed, and finally Kendrick.

Esha stood on Kendrick's back before doing a forward somersault to land on the ground beside him. She walked to stand before the dragons. As she eyed her fellow elves, Rhi appeared beside her. Rhi created an iridescent orb of magic between her hands and glared at the Rangers.

"Take a look," Esha told the elves. "Take a hard look at the dragons before you. Now, look behind them in the distance. Do you see the dark spot? That's not a cloud. That's more dragons. Coming here. No one wants a war. If they did, they would've killed you the moment you crossed into Idrias."

Kendrick shifted, as did Eurwen, Vaughn, and then Con, showing the elves that others had Kendrick's ability.

"I came uninvited to your land with peaceful intentions," Kendrick said. "You've come uninvited to ours with violent ones. This is your one and only warning."

Eurwen stepped forward then. "The next time anyone comes here uninvited, there will be consequences."

"The same goes for any of you," an elf shouted.

Con shrugged. "Agreed. Now, I think it's time you return to your land."

Esha held her breath until the Rangers turned and retraced their steps. Only when she was sure they were gone did she turn to Kendrick. "It worked," she said as she threw her arms around him.

"Of course, it did. We're brilliant, did you no' know?" he teased before giving her a quick kiss.

Eurwen approached. "Thank you, Esha. It must have been hard to leave your home. What you did took a lot of bravery."

"Agreed," Rhi said with a nod.

Vaughn grinned at her. "I hope one day the elves know what you and Savita did to save them."

"Oh, I think Dain will make sure of that," Kendrick said.

Con looked toward Shecrish. "We thwarted a war. That is cause for celebration." He turned to look between Esha and Kendrick. "The two of you could use a wee break. Besides, Esha hasn't met everyone yet. They're waiting for us at Cairnkeep."

"We wouldna miss it," Kendrick said as he smiled at her.

Esha couldn't wait to see Cairnkeep. "That sounds delightful."

"I'll send someone to take your place here," Vaughn said.

After the others had left, Esha and Kendrick walked hand in hand back to the mountain and their yurt. She thought it a funny word, but she enjoyed the structure.

"Just tell me when you're ready," he said.

She glanced at him. "Ready for what?"

"To be mated."

"I thought we were."

"You're my mate, but there's a mating ceremony. It's quite elaborate."

She tried to imagine what that was. "We have marriage ceremonies. They're simple and can be done anywhere, anytime, by anyone."

"Ah. This is a bit different. Con officiates them. And you'll get a tattoo."

That intrigued her. "Do I get to choose what it is?"

"Nay," he said with a grin as he met her gaze. "It'll be the same one every mate has."

"Is it pretty?"

That made him laugh. "I think so. It'll be on your upper left arm."

"Is that all that happens?"

"You get to pick what you wear."

Esha laughed out loud. "Well, I should hope so."

"And after, you'll live for as long as I do."

She halted and stared at him with wide eyes. "Can you repeat that?"

"A Dragon King's mate lives for as long as he does."

"Are you telling me I can't be killed?"

His lips curved in a smile. "That's what I'm saying."

"Oh. I don't think I'm interested in that," she teased, but she couldn't hold a straight face.

Kendrick playfully grabbed for her. She squealed as she tried to run away, but he caught her in his arms. They laughed as they tumbled to the ground. He rolled on top of her and gazed at her with passion burning in his green eyes.

This was her Dragon King, her mate. She hadn't thought she could love anyone as much as she loved him. Esha reached up and pulled his head down for a scorching kiss—and the pleasure that awaited her in his arms.

* * * *

"She's safe. I saw her with Kendrick," Dain said as he stood in Savita's tent in Flamefall.

The Reader nodded slowly. "Does she look happy?"

"Very."

"And there was no bloodshed? The dragons didn't attack?"

Dain held back his grin. "They didn't attack the elves. I give the Rangers credit for not running at the sight of them. I would have. It was...impressive."

"Fools. Every last one of them."

"They were following orders."

She sneered. "Not all of them. Some asked to join the cause."

Dain clasped his hands behind his back. "Did you get anything today?"

"Nothing concrete," she said, agitation deepening her voice. "Yet. I suspect I know who sent the nightwraith after my sister. This particular Conclave member is...devious. I'll get the proof I need, though."

"We're treading on dangerous ground."

Savita shoved her long, tawny hair over her shoulder. "No one suspects us."

"Let's keep it that way."

"What about your lead?"

"I'm about to head there now. I'll contact you when I have something."

Savita stepped toward him. "Thank you for helping me."

"I'm helping me," he said before calling the shadows to him.

* * * *

Stonemore

Merrill looked west. He'd stopped trying to reach his brethren weeks ago. He should be angrier than he was that they hadn't tried to contact him. Maybe it was for the best. He wasn't the same dragon he had been. There was only so much a man could take, and he had reached his limit.

He'd actually reached it long ago, but he had kept a firm handle on it. While at Stonemore, he'd just stopped caring. The residents of Zora might not know the history of the dragons, which meant they couldn't know that they were close to repeating the past. But he knew. So did the other Kings.

He was tired of innocents dying, tired of pretending to be something he wasn't.

The mortals on Zora were just as brash and arrogant as those on Earth. He swung his head to the side to look at Villette, who lay naked beneath the covers of their bed. He couldn't explain why he remained with her. She hid many things, and he intended to get to each of them in time.

She stretched and opened her eyes, searching until she found him at the window. "Still nothing from your friends?"

Merrill shook his head.

She flung back the covers, exposing her lush, sensual body. "Let me take your mind off it."

He strode to her as she smiled triumphantly. Merrill grabbed her wrists when she reached for him and pinned them above her head before settling between her legs. Her eyes glowed with excitement.

"Yes," she whispered urgently.

When he didn't move, she lifted her hips and ground against him. The light from the fire in the hearth danced along the scarred side of her face. She was using him. He was certain of that. But then again, he was using her, too. Stonemore held many secrets, and he intended to uncover each and every one.

She pouted up at him, then leaned forward to lick his nipple. "What do you want, lover?"

That would come soon enough. For now...

He thrust into her, burying himself deep.

And her gasp turned into a moan.

* * * *

Merrill and the rest of the Dragon Kings will return in DRAGON ARISEN, coming June 2023.

* * * *

Also from 1001 Dark Nights and Donna Grant, discover Dragon Unbound, Dragon Revealed, Dragon Lost, Dragon Claimed, Dragon Night, Dragon Burn, Dragon Fever, and Dragon King.

Sign up for the 1001 Dark Nights Newsletter
and be entered to win a Tiffany Key necklace.

There's a contest every month!

Go to www.1001DarkNights.com to subscribe.

**As a bonus, all subscribers can download
FIVE FREE exclusive books!**

Discover 1001 Dark Nights Collection Ten

DRAGON LOVER by Donna Grant
A Dragon Kings Novella

KEEPING YOU by Aurora Rose Reynolds
An Until Him/Her Novella

HAPPILY EVER NEVER by Carrie Ann Ryan
A Montgomery Ink Legacy Novella

DESTINED FOR ME by Corinne Michaels
A Come Back for Me/Say You'll Stay Crossover

MADAM ALANA by Audrey Carlan
A Marriage Auction Novella

DIRTY FILTHY BILLIONAIRE by Laurelin Paige
A Dirty Universe Novella

HIDE AND SEEK by Laura Kaye
A Blasphemy Novella

TANGLED WITH YOU by J. Kenner
A Stark Security Novella

TEMPTED by Lexi Blake
A Masters and Mercenaries Novella

THE DANDELION DIARY by Devney Perry
A Maysen Jar Novella

CHERRY LANE by Kristen Proby
A Huckleberry Bay Novella

THE GRAVE ROBBER by Darynda Jones
A Charley Davidson Novella

CRY OF THE BANSHEE by Heather Graham
A Krewe of Hunters Novella

DARKEST NEED by Rachel Van Dyken
A Dark Ones Novella

CHRISTMAS IN CAPE MAY by Jennifer Probst
A Sunshine Sisters Novella

A VAMPIRE'S MATE by Rebecca Zanetti
A Dark Protectors/Rebels Novella

WHERE IT BEGINS by Helena Hunting
A Pucked Novella

Also from Blue Box Press

THE MARRIAGE AUCTION by Audrey Carlan
Season One, Volume One
Season One, Volume Two
Season One, Volume Three
Season One, Volume Four

THE JEWELER OF STOLEN DREAMS by M.J. Rose

LOVE ON THE BYLINE by Xio Axelrod
A Plays and Players Novel

SAPPHIRE STORM by Christopher Rice writing as C. Travis Rice
A Sapphire Cove Novel

ATLAS: THE STORY OF PA SALT by Lucinda Riley and Harry
Whittaker

A SOUL OF ASH AND BLOOD by Jennifer L. Armentrout
A Blood and Ash Novel

FIGHTING THE PULL by Kristen Ashley
A River Rain Novel

VISIONS OF FLESH AND BLOOD by Jennifer L. Armentrout and
Rayvn Salvador
A Blood and Ash/Flesh and Fire Compendium

A FIRE IN THE FLESH by Jennifer L. Armentrout
A Flesh and Fire Novel

Discover More Donna Grant

Dragon Unbound
A Dragon Kings Novella

He's never been tempted...until her.

Sexy. Mysterious. Dangerous. He's an immortal Dragon King bound by ancient rules and eternal magic. Cullen has one objective: find and destroy the evil that threatens the new home of the dragons. Just when he's closing in, he's ambushed and finds a stunning warrior woman fighting alongside him. No amount of magic could prepare him for the beguiling lass who spurns his advances and defies him.

From the moment Tamlyn takes a stand against her kind, she's had to fight one perilous battle after another. Staying alive in an endless struggle, and the lines between good and evil are blurred with every encounter. She's always stood alone—until she comes to the aid of an irresistibly handsome stranger. Cullen will force her to face truths she's been running from...even as enemies plot to destroy them both.

* * * *

Dragon Revealed
A Dragon Kings Novella

The capture of a Dragon King is cause for celebration. Jeyra never dreamed she would actually face one of the creatures who destroyed her home. But the longer she's around him, the more she finds herself gravitating to him. All it takes is one reckless kiss that unleashes desires and the truth that has been hidden from her to set them both on a course that could be the end of them.

Varek, King of Lichens, has known nothing but a life with magic. Until he finds himself on a different realm unable to call up his powers. Worse, he's in shackles with no memory of how it happened. When he sees an enthralling woman who leaves him speechless, he believes he can charm her to free him. The more she rebuffs him, the more he craves her, igniting a dangerous passion between them. Can he protect the woman he's fallen for while uncovering the truth – or will peril that neither see coming tear them apart?

* * * *

Dragon Lost
A Dark Kings Novella

Destinies can't be ignored. No one knows that better than Annita. For as long as she can remember, it's been foretold she would find a dragon. A real-life dragon. She's beginning to think it was all some kind of mistake until she's swimming in one of the many caves around the island and discovers none other than a dragon. There is no fear as she approaches, utterly transfixed at the sight of the creature. Then he shifts into the shape of a thoroughly gorgeous man who spears her with bright blue eyes. In that instant, she knows her destiny has arrived. And the dragon holds the key to everything.

All Royden wanted was to find an item his brother buried when they were children. It was supposed to be a quick and simple trip, but he should've known nothing would be easy with enemies like the Dragon Kings have. Royden has no choice but to trust the beguiling woman who tempts him like no other. And in doing so, they unleash a love so strong, so pure that nothing can hold it back.

* * * *

Dragon Claimed
A Dark Kings Novella

Born to rule the skies as a Dragon King with power and magic, Cináed hides his true identity in the mountains of Scotland with the rest of his brethren. But there is no respite for them as they protect the planet and the human occupants from threats. However, a new, more dangerous enemy has targeted the Kings. One that will stop at nothing until dragons are gone forever. But Cináed discovers a woman from a powerful, ancient Druid bloodline who might have a connection to this new foe.

Solitude is sanctuary for Gemma. Her young life was upended one stormy night when her family disappears, leaving her utterly alone. She learned to depend solely on herself from then on. But no matter where she goes she feels...lost. As if she missed the path she was supposed to take. Everything changes when she backs into the most dangerously seductive man she's ever laid eyes. Gemma surrenders to the all-consuming attraction and the wild, impossible love that could destroy them both – and finds her path amid magic and dragons.

* * * *

Dragon Night
A Dark Kings Novella

Governed by honor and ruled by desire

There has never been a hunt that Dorian has lost. With his sights set on a relic the Dragon Kings need to battle an ancient foe, he won't let anything stand in his way – especially not the beautiful owner. Alexandra is smart and cautious. Yet the attraction between them is impossible to deny – or ignore. But is it a road Dorian dares to travel down again?

With her vast family fortune, Alexandra Sheridan is never without suitors. No one is more surprised than she when the charming, devilish Scotsman snags her attention. But the secrets Dorian holds is like a wall between them until one fateful night when he shares everything. In his arms she finds passion like no other – and a love that will transcend time. But can she give her heart to a dragon??

* * * *

Dragon Burn
A Dark Kings Novella

Marked by passion

A promise made eons ago sends Sebastian to Italy on the hunt to find an enemy. His quarry proves difficult to locate, but there is someone who can point him in the right direction – a woman as frigid as the north. Using every seductive skill he's acquired over his immortal life, his seduction begins. Until he discovers that the passion he stirs within her makes him burn for more…

Gianna Santini has one love in her life – work. A disastrous failed marriage was evidence enough to realize she was better off on her own. That is until a handsome Scot strolled into her life and literally swept her off her feet. She is unprepared for the blazing passion between them or the truth he exposes. But as her world begins to unravel, she realizes the only one she can depend on is the very one destroying everything - a Dragon King.

* * * *

Dragon Fever
A Dark Kings Novella

A yearning that won't be denied

Rachel Marek is a journalist with a plan. She intends to expose the truth about dragons to the world – and her target is within sight. Nothing matters but getting the truth, especially not the ruggedly handsome, roguishly thrilling Highlander who oozes danger and charm. And when she finds the truth that shatters her faith, she'll have to trust her heart to the very man who can crush it…

A legend in the flesh

Suave, dashing Asher is more than just a man. He's a Dragon King – a being who has roamed this planet since the beginning of time. With everything on the line, Asher must choose to trust an enemy in the form of an all too alluring woman whose tenacity and passion captivate him. Together, Asher and Rachel must fight for their lives – and their love – before an old enemy destroys them both…

* * * *

Dragon King
A Dark Kings Novella

A Woman on A Mission

Grace Clark has always done things safe. She's never colored outside of the law, but she has a book due and has found the perfect spot to break through her writer's block. Or so she thinks. Right up until Arian suddenly appears and tries to force her away from the mountain. Unaware of the war she just stumbled into, Grace doesn't just discover the perfect place to write, she finds Arian - the most gorgeous, enticing, mysterious man she's ever met.

A King with a Purpose

Arian is a Dragon King who has slept away centuries in his cave. Recently woken, he's about to leave his mountain to join his brethren in a war when he's alerted that someone has crossed onto Dreagan. He's ready to fight...until he sees the woman. She's innocent and mortal - and she sets his blood aflame. He recognizes the danger approaching her just as the dragon within him demands he claim her for his own...

Iron Ember

Skye Druids Book 1
By Donna Grant

Delve into the thrilling first installment of the all-new Skye Druids series by *New York Times* bestselling author Donna Grant, where magic reigns and danger abounds.

Skye isn't just an island. It's a home. A refuge. But not to Elodie MacLean. Not anymore. Tragedy tore her world apart and then took the one thing she felt made her whole. She vowed she'd never return, but that's exactly where she ends up. Now, surrounded by the ghosts of her past, Elodie must navigate her version of Hell and try to make peace with herself and her family. But someone or something doesn't want her on Skye, and she finds herself attacked—and this time not by her personal demons.

Scott Ryan has a mission: uncover who has been killing Druids and why. When his quest takes him to the beautiful Isle of Skye, he doesn't think anything could captivate him more than the land itself—until he lays eyes on the breathtaking and confident beauty his leader sent him to find. However, it's clear that she has trust issues, and he can't reveal his plans—at least, not yet. But he's always been sure of his ability to sway a person, and she's a challenge he's more than happy to accept, especially when he finds he will do anything to protect her.

With so much history and so many secrets, victory is anything but guaranteed for the couple and their allies. And the forces at work, those who wish to rule the Scottish isle and all those who reside there, have a plan that nobody will see coming

* * * *

Chapter One

She was back.

It was the last place she wanted to be but the only place she had to run to.

Elodie threw open the curtains. Dust danced in the air, the sunlight catching it. She stared out the dirty window to the sea beyond. Skye. The home she'd proclaimed she would never leave because she loved it so fiercely.

It was also the place she had sworn to never return to.

And yet, here she was.

"Bloody hell," she murmured as she turned her back to the window and looked over what remained of the furniture from her parents' cottage.

Her gaze slid to the hearth where echoes of children's laughter clung to the stones. Her mother had made the best hot cocoa. After playing for hours outside in the winter, Elodie, her elder sister, Edie, and her brother, Elias, would sit before the fire with steaming cups of cocoa and her grandmother's strawberry scones.

Elodie squeezed her eyes shut. She wanted to hold onto the lighthearted memories, but the other ones were always on their heels—the ones that had altered all their lives, throwing them into chaos.

She blew out a breath and focused on the clutter and mess before her. The dust was so thick that she knew she would end up with respiratory problems for days if she didn't take precautions. And it wasn't as if she could use magic to prevent it.

Returning to Skye was like walking through one of Dante's nine circles of Hell. Elodie didn't know how she would survive being back on the island. If only she'd had somewhere else to go. *Anywhere* else. If she still believed, she would think Skye had interfered and brought her back.

"If that's the case, then my magic wouldn't be gone, now would it?"

It was hard not to be bitter and angry about her life. She owned her decisions, but she had been on a different path. Then, everything had imploded with the force of a nuclear explosion.

When she looked around after, everyone just went about their lives as if her family hadn't been rocked to its core. As if she and her siblings hadn't had their blinders ripped off with such force that it'd changed all three of them in one heartbeat—their innocence gone in the blink of an eye.

Corann had tried to help, but the old Druid hadn't been able to reach any of them. And Elias had left. Elodie still hadn't forgiven him for leaving her and Edie to navigate the churning waters of their society. Elodie might have been the youngest, but she was the one who'd ended up taking care of Edie. Her sister had the kind, gentle spirit of their mother. Elodie had lashed out and turned to drinking and drugs, but Edie had gone into herself.

Elodie walked through the main area of the cottage and past the kitchen to the hallway. Pictures of their family still hung on the walls. Snapshots of a happy life that had hidden the rot beneath. She stopped at one where Edie smiled brightly with a cake and lit candles before her. Maybe Elodie hadn't been the one to take care of Edie. They had leaned on each other, clinging to one another and struggling to keep their heads above water. It was only because of her sister that Elodie hadn't sunk too deeply into the hard life. She'd known she had to be there for Edie. And in the end, they'd kept each other afloat.

Until Elodie hadn't been able to stay another minute on Skye.

Fifteen years. It seemed like a lifetime, but it was much too soon to be back. Nothing would keep her on Skye longer than necessary this time. Not her sister. Nothing. Skye had annihilated her family. It had destroyed her. How Edie could remain on the isle was a mystery. And Elias? All Elodie could hope for was that her brother had found some semblance of happiness. They all deserved it.

Elodie forced herself to walk to each room, but she couldn't manage to go inside her parents'. She stood before the closed door as screams and shouts from that horrible day filled her head. Elodie backed away and turned on her heel. How in the world would she stay in the cottage? Sleep just feet from where it'd all happened.

"I can't," she stated with a shake of her head.

Elodie grabbed her purse and the single bag that held her measly belongings and started for the door. Then she remembered *why* she was on Skye.

"Fuck!" she yelled and fought the sudden urge to release the scream of frustration that welled up.

She wasn't a crier, but everyone had their breaking point. She forced the tears back and dropped her bags. The only way to get on with her life was to take her sister's offer. All Elodie had to do was clean up the cottage so they could sell it. It was a good deal. Elodie had the place to herself instead of sleeping on the sofa at Edie's crowded house with her sister's kids and husband. And all without having to pay any sort of rent.

Since Elodie was homeless and jobless and had less than two hundred pounds to her name, it really was a blessing. At least she'd thought that until she arrived on Skye. Even driving around the island had made her chest constrict. Her anxiety rose with every mile. Then she'd arrived at the cottage. It had taken Elodie half an hour to work up the courage to actually walk inside.

"Maybe I deserve this torture," she said aloud. "I didn't exactly live a good life."

This was supposed to be her chance to start over. To travel the path she'd been on before she got derailed.

"Fine. Let's do this."

She opened the door, then went to all the windows and opened them despite the frigid temperatures and the threat of rain. The dust had to go somewhere, and the sooner she got it out of the house, the better. Elodie started in the bedroom she had once shared with her sister. She carefully folded the bed linens from each twin bed and dumped them outside. Thankfully, Edie had given her fresh sheets, pillows, and blankets.

Next, she found an old towel and used some cleaner to wipe down the walls and window, sweeping the cobwebs from the corners before vacuuming the carpet. Only then did she bring in her bag and purse.

Elodie wiped her face with her arm and made her way to the main area. Someone had placed sheets over the furniture. She slowly and carefully folded them, but there was so much dust that some still escaped. The pile joined the bed linens outside. On her way back inside, she smiled as she saw the dust wafting out the windows. Hopefully, most of it would land outside instead of back in the house.

The smallish living area didn't take long to wipe down. The windows would take more than one cleaning. She didn't want to touch the outside yet. That was a whole other matter entirely. Her first priority was to get the inside clean enough that she could locate any repairs that needed to be addressed. Only after she did that would she tackle the outside.

The old cottage was too quiet. Elodie pulled out her phone and put on her favorite playlist as she went back to cleaning. She kept moving, which helped to keep her warm. There was a brief shower, but she didn't bother closing the windows. The house needed to be aired out to get rid of the musty smell. She suddenly froze, the hairs on the back of her neck lifting. Slowly, she straightened from scrubbing the bathroom counter and looked at the doorway. No one was there. At least no one she could see.

A chill raced down her spine. With the sponge still in her gloved hands, she walked into the hallway. She glanced at her parents' room, then looked the other way. Elodie slowly made her way to the kitchen. Her gaze landed on a tall, gorgeous man with black and silver hair, standing next to a pretty female with red hair.

The man was a Fae. It seemed there was no escaping them anywhere, but they hadn't been allowed on Skye in decades. At least as far as she knew. What was he doing back?

"Hi," the woman said.

Elodie swung her gaze to the female. She looked close to Elodie's age, and something about her seemed familiar.

"You don't remember me, do you?" the woman asked with a smile.

Elodie shook her head. It was unnerving that people already knew she was on the isle. Worse that they remembered her when she had done everything to forget Skye and everyone on it. "I don't."

"You've been gone awhile. I'm Rhona."

In an instant, Elodie remembered Rhona and her cousin, Sorcha. They used to come over occasionally. She had always liked both girls. Elodie glanced at the floor, slightly embarrassed for the harsh welcome she had given them. "Of course."

Rhona looked at the man beside her, love shining in her eyes. "This is Balladyn."

"A Fae," Elodie said before she could stop herself.

Balladyn inclined his head of long hair. His eyes were silver, but she saw a ring of red around them. "Reaper, actually." His voice had an Irish lilt.

Reaper. Elodie wasn't sure what that meant.

"We wanted to welcome you back and see if you needed anything," Rhona said.

Elodie shifted her feet nervously. Did they know she'd lost her magic? "That wasn't necessary."

"You're one of us," Rhona said with a soft look. "We look after our own."

Resentment threatened to choke Elodie, and she had to remind herself that she shouldn't direct her anger at Rhona. She hadn't been any older than Elodie back then. Corann was a different matter. "Corann sent you?"

A frown moved over Rhona's face so quickly that Elodie almost missed it. "We lost Corann. I've taken his place."

"Oh." Damn. She should've had Edie bring her up to date on things. Then again, Elodie hadn't wanted to talk to any Druids, so she had made sure not to take an interest in anything. "Honestly, I won't be here long. As soon as I get the place fixed up and sold, I'm leaving."

Rhona's green eyes narrowed slightly. "That's a pity. We could use you."

No one ever had use for her. Elodie glanced at Balladyn to see that the Reaper's gaze hadn't moved from her. It was unnerving to have him watch her in such a way, and yet she didn't feel threatened. "It's for the best."

"Why don't you come for tea later this week? We can catch up," Rhona said.

Elodie's plan to keep to herself was rapidly disintegrating. She liked Rhona—or at least the person she had once been. It wasn't in Elodie's nature to be outright rude, but Rhona would likely ask questions that Elodie wasn't prepared to answer. And she was tired of lying. "I'm no–"

"Please don't decline. Think it over." Rhona smiled. "Please."

Well, bugger it. "I'll consider it."

Rhona's smile was huge. "Great. And if you need any help, we can get this place together quickly."

The offer was so tempting that Elodie nearly took it. If they did, she could leave Skye that much quicker. However, if she agreed to Rhona's offer, it would inevitably lead to those pesky questions she was intent on dodging. "Thanks, but I've already made good headway today."

"At the very least, let me fix the leaking roof," Balladyn said.

Her gaze snapped to him. The roof was leaking? She glanced around but didn't hear any dripping. Then a drop landed on top of her head. This might be a bigger project than she'd thought. She faced him and forced her tight lips into a smile as her stomach churned with anxiety. "I would appreciate that."

"It's done," he said with a bow of his head.

"Thank you."

Rhona flashed another smile. "It's good to have you back. I hope you'll consider the tea."

Elodie held her smile until the two of them suddenly disappeared. She blinked and frowned. Balladyn must have teleported them out. At least the leak was fixed. She looked up at the ceiling and spotted the water damage.

"I'm going to be here forever," she grumbled.

About Donna Grant

New York Times and *USA Today* bestselling author Donna Grant has been praised for her "totally addictive" and "unique and sensual" stories. Her latest acclaimed series, Dragon Kings, features a thrilling combination of dragons, Fae, and immortal Highlanders who are dark, dangerous, and irresistible. She lives with an assortment of animals in Texas.

Visit Donna at
www.DonnaGrant.com
www.MotherOfDragonsBooks.com

Discover 1001 Dark Nights

by Rebecca Zanetti ~ DIRTY WICKED by Shayla Black ~ THE ONLY ONE by Lauren Blakely ~ SWEET SURRENDER by Liliana Hart

COLLECTION FOUR

ROCK CHICK REAWAKENING by Kristen Ashley ~ ADORING INK by Carrie Ann Ryan ~ SWEET RIVALRY by K. Bromberg ~ SHADE'S LADY by Joanna Wylde ~ RAZR by Larissa Ione ~ ARRANGED by Lexi Blake ~ TANGLED by Rebecca Zanetti ~ HOLD ME by J. Kenner ~ SOMEHOW, SOME WAY by Jennifer Probst ~ TOO CLOSE TO CALL by Tessa Bailey ~ HUNTED by Elisabeth Naughton ~ EYES ON YOU by Laura Kaye ~ BLADE by Alexandra Ivy/Laura Wright ~ DRAGON BURN by Donna Grant ~ TRIPPED OUT by Lorelei James ~ STUD FINDER by Lauren Blakely ~ MIDNIGHT UNLEASHED by Lara Adrian ~ HALLOW BE THE HAUNT by Heather Graham ~ DIRTY FILTHY FIX by Laurelin Paige ~ THE BED MATE by Kendall Ryan ~ NIGHT GAMES by CD Reiss ~ NO RESERVATIONS by Kristen Proby ~ DAWN OF SURRENDER by Liliana Hart

COLLECTION FIVE

BLAZE ERUPTING by Rebecca Zanetti ~ ROUGH RIDE by Kristen Ashley ~ HAWKYN by Larissa Ione ~ RIDE DIRTY by Laura Kaye ~ ROME'S CHANCE by Joanna Wylde ~ THE MARRIAGE ARRANGEMENT by Jennifer Probst ~ SURRENDER by Elisabeth Naughton ~ INKED NIGHTS by Carrie Ann Ryan ~ ENVY by Rachel Van Dyken ~ PROTECTED by Lexi Blake ~ THE PRINCE by Jennifer L. Armentrout ~ PLEASE ME by J. Kenner ~ WOUND TIGHT by Lorelei James ~ STRONG by Kylie Scott ~ DRAGON NIGHT by Donna Grant ~ TEMPTING BROOKE by Kristen Proby ~ HAUNTED BE THE HOLIDAYS by Heather Graham ~ CONTROL by K. Bromberg ~ HUNKY HEARTBREAKER by Kendall Ryan ~ THE DARKEST CAPTIVE by Gena Showalter

COLLECTION SIX

DRAGON CLAIMED by Donna Grant ~ ASHES TO INK by Carrie Ann Ryan ~ ENSNARED by Elisabeth Naughton ~ EVERMORE by Corinne Michaels ~ VENGEANCE by Rebecca Zanetti ~ ELI'S TRIUMPH by Joanna Wylde ~ CIPHER by Larissa Ione ~ RESCUING MACIE by Susan Stoker ~ ENCHANTED by Lexi Blake ~ TAKE THE BRIDE by Carly Phillips ~ INDULGE ME by J. Kenner ~ THE KING by Jennifer L. Armentrout ~ QUIET MAN by Kristen Ashley ~ ABANDON by Rachel Van Dyken ~ THE OPEN DOOR by Laurelin Paige ~ CLOSER by Kylie Scott ~ SOMETHING JUST LIKE THIS by Jennifer Probst ~ BLOOD NIGHT by Heather Graham ~ TWIST OF FATE by Jill Shalvis ~ MORE THAN PLEASURE YOU by Shayla Black ~ WONDER WITH ME by Kristen Proby ~ THE DARKEST ASSASSIN by Gena Showalter

COLLECTION SEVEN
THE BISHOP by Skye Warren ~ TAKEN WITH YOU by Carrie Ann Ryan ~ DRAGON LOST by Donna Grant ~ SEXY LOVE by Carly Phillips ~ PROVOKE by Rachel Van Dyken ~ RAFE by Sawyer Bennett ~ THE NAUGHTY PRINCESS by Claire Contreras ~ THE GRAVEYARD SHIFT by Darynda Jones ~ CHARMED by Lexi Blake ~ SACRIFICE OF DARKNESS by Alexandra Ivy ~ THE QUEEN by Jen Armentrout ~ BEGIN AGAIN by Jennifer Probst ~ VIXEN by Rebecca Zanetti ~ SLASH by Laurelin Paige ~ THE DEAD HEAT OF SUMMER by Heather Graham ~ WILD FIRE by Kristen Ashley ~ MORE THAN PROTECT YOU by Shayla Black ~ LOVE SONG by Kylie Scott ~ CHERISH ME by J. Kenner ~ SHINE WITH ME by Kristen Proby

COLLECTION EIGHT
DRAGON REVEALED by Donna Grant ~ CAPTURED IN INK by Carrie Ann Ryan ~ SECURING JANE by Susan Stoker ~ WILD WIND by Kristen Ashley ~ DARE TO TEASE by Carly Phillips ~ VAMPIRE by Rebecca Zanetti ~ MAFIA KING by Rachel Van Dyken ~ THE GRAVEDIGGER'S SON by Darynda Jones ~ FINALE by Skye Warren ~ MEMORIES OF YOU by J. Kenner ~ SLAYED BY DARKNESS by Alexandra Ivy ~ TREASURED by Lexi Blake ~ THE DAREDEVIL by Dylan Allen ~ BOND OF DESTINY by Larissa Ione ~ MORE THAN POSSESS YOU by Shayla Black ~ HAUNTED HOUSE by Heather Graham ~ MAN FOR ME by Laurelin Paige ~ THE RHYTHM METHOD by Kylie Scott ~ JONAH BENNETT by Tijan ~ CHANGE WITH ME by Kristen Proby ~ THE DARKEST DESTINY by Gena Showalter

COLLECTION NINE
DRAGON UNBOUND by Donna Grant ~ NOTHING BUT INK by Carrie Ann Ryan ~ THE MASTERMIND by Dylan Allen ~ JUST ONE

WISH by Carly Phillips ~ BEHIND CLOSED DOORS by Skye Warren ~ GOSSAMER IN THE DARKNESS by Kristen Ashley ~ THE CLOSE-UP by Kennedy Ryan ~ DELIGHTED by Lexi Blake ~ THE GRAVESIDE BAR AND GRILL by Darynda Jones ~ THE ANTI-FAN AND THE IDOL by Rachel Van Dyken ~ CHARMED BY YOU by J. Kenner ~ DESCEND TO DARKNESS by Heather Graham~ BOND OF PASSION by Larissa Ione ~ JUST WHAT I NEEDED by Kylie Scott

Discover Blue Box Press

TAME ME by J. Kenner ~ TEMPT ME by J. Kenner ~ DAMIEN by J. Kenner ~ TEASE ME by J. Kenner ~ REAPER by Larissa Ione ~ THE SURRENDER GATE by Christopher Rice ~ SERVICING THE TARGET by Cherise Sinclair ~ THE LAKE OF LEARNING by Steve Berry and M.J. Rose ~ THE MUSEUM OF MYSTERIES by Steve Berry and M.J. Rose ~ TEASE ME by J. Kenner ~ FROM BLOOD AND ASH by Jennifer L. Armentrout ~ QUEEN MOVE by Kennedy Ryan ~ THE HOUSE OF LONG AGO by Steve Berry and M.J. Rose ~ THE BUTTERFLY ROOM by Lucinda Riley ~ A KINGDOM OF FLESH AND FIRE by Jennifer L. Armentrout ~ THE LAST TIARA by M.J. Rose ~ THE CROWN OF GILDED BONES by Jennifer L. Armentrout ~ THE MISSING SISTER by Lucinda Riley ~ THE END OF FOREVER by Steve Berry and M.J. Rose ~ THE STEAL by C. W. Gortner and M.J. Rose ~ CHASING SERENITY by Kristen Ashley ~ A SHADOW IN THE EMBER by Jennifer L. Armentrout ~ THE BAIT by C.W. Gortner and M.J. Rose ~ THE FASHION ORPHANS by Randy Susan Meyers and M.J. Rose ~ TAKING THE LEAP by Kristen Ashley ~ SAPPHIRE SUNSET by Christopher Rice writing C. Travis Rice ~ THE WAR OF TWO QUEENS by Jennifer L. Armentrout ~ THE MURDERS AT FLEAT HOUSE by Lucinda Riley ~ THE HEIST by C.W. Gortner and M.J. Rose ~ SAPPHIRE SPRING by Christopher Rice writing as C. Travis Rice ~ MAKING THE MATCH by Kristen Ashley ~ A LIGHT IN THE FLAME by Jennifer L.

On Behalf of 1001 Dark Nights,

Liz Berry, M.J. Rose, and Jillian Stein would like to thank ~

Steve Berry
Doug Scofield
Benjamin Stein
Kim Guidroz
Social Butterfly PR
Asha Hossain
Chris Graham
Chelle Olson
Kasi Alexander
Jessica Saunders
Dylan Stockton
Kate Boggs
Richard Blake
and Simon Lipskar

Printed in Great Britain
by Amazon

16662634R00114